*Alex's eyes met hers briefly before he looked away.*

And once again P. J. felt that spark of awareness and attraction.

She had to get control of herself and quit acting like a silly teenager.

On the one hand, the best thing would be to give Alex Noble a wide berth. A real wide berth. On the other hand, that wouldn't be the best thing for HuntCom.

In fact, she should probably keep a close eye on him. Make sure he was actually doing the job he'd been hired to do.

Maybe she was just paranoid about Alex because he was so attractive. Face it, she chided herself, you've been exposed to too many good-looking, self-centered, arrogant men in your lifetime and now you think they're *all* like that.

Maybe Alex Noble would prove to be the exception....

Dear Reader,

The whole time I was writing this book, I kept thinking how lucky P.J. was, and she didn't even know it. After all, what young woman *wouldn't* want to meet and fall in love with a billionaire? Especially one as handsome and wonderful as Alex. But, as loyal readers of romance know, the course of true love never runs smoothly. And the story of P.J. and Alex is no exception.

I hope you enjoy reading their story as much as I enjoyed writing it. And I hope you're as anxious to read Gray's story (coming next) as I am. The Hunt brothers really wormed their way into my heart, and I can't wait to find out what happens next.

As always, thank you for your faithful readership. You are all wonderful and very much appreciated.

Warmly,

*Patricia Kay*

# THE BILLIONAIRE
# AND HIS BOSS

## *PATRICIA KAY*

Silhouette®

SPECIAL EDITION®

Published by Silhouette Books

America's Publisher of Contemporary Romance

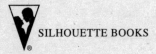

SILHOUETTE BOOKS

ISBN-13: 978-0-373-28123-7
ISBN-10:     0-373-28123-4

THE BILLIONAIRE AND HIS BOSS

---

*PATRICIA KAY,*

formerly writing as Trisha Alexander, is the *USA TODAY* bestselling author of more than thirty contemporary romances. She lives in Houston, Texas. To learn more about her, visit her Web site at www.patriciakay.com.

This one's for Gail, with a huge thank-you
for all the years of encouragement and friendship.

## Prologue

*Mid-July, The Hunt Mansion*

Harrison Hunt, founder and CEO of HuntCom, sat behind his enormous mahogany desk in the library of the behemoth he called home and looked from one to the other of his sons. "Four sons and not a marriage among you." He shook his head in obvious dismay. "I've never thought much about my legacy, nor about having grandchildren to carry on the Hunt name. But my heart attack made me face some hard truths. I could have died. I could die tomorrow."

His face was grimly intent as he continued. "I finally realized that left to your own devices, you four never *will* get married, which means I'll never have grandchildren. Well, I don't intend to leave the future of this family to chance any longer."

His eyes bored into theirs. "You have a year. One year. By the end of that time, each of you will not only be married, you will either already have a child or your wife will be expecting one."

Alex Hunt stared at his father. He couldn't believe what he was hearing, and he could see from the expressions on the faces of his brothers that they felt the same way. Was this a joke? Had that heart attack Harry'd had affected his brain?

"And if any one of you refuses," Harry continued flatly, ignoring the disbelief in their faces, "you'll all lose your positions in HuntCom…and the perks you love so much."

"You can't be serious," Gray, the oldest at forty-two, finally said.

"I'm deadly serious."

J.T., two years older than Alex at thirty-eight, broke the brief, shocked silence. "How will you run the company if we refuse to do what you want?" He reminded their father of the expansions taking place in Seattle and in their Delhi facility. "Construction delays alone would cost HuntCom a fortune."

But Harry didn't budge. He said it didn't matter about the current projects, because if they didn't agree to do what he was demanding, he would sell the entire HuntCom empire, including the ranch Justin loved so much, the island that was J.T.'s passion, and the foundation that meant so much to Alex. Gray cared about everything. He'd been second-in-command to Harry ever since graduating from college and he fully expected to move into the president's spot when Harry finally retired.

"Before I die," Harry continued relentlessly, "I mean to see each of you settled, and with a family started. I want you married to decent women who'll make good wives and mothers." He paused for a moment, then added, "And the women you marry have to win Cornelia's approval."

"Does Aunt Cornelia know about this?" Justin, who was the youngest brother at thirty-four, asked in disbelief.

Alex also had a hard time believing their sensible honorary aunt would go along with such a nutty scheme.

"Not yet," Harry admitted.

Alex knew his relief was shared by his brothers. When Cornelia learned about Harry's plan, she'd put a stop to it. In fact, she was the *only* one capable of talking Harry out of anything. He would listen to her.

"So," Justin said, "Let me see if I've got this straight. Each of us has to agree to marry and produce a kid within a year—"

"*All* of you have to agree," Harry interrupted. "All four of you. If one refuses, everyone loses, and life as you've known it—your jobs, the HuntCom holdings you each value so much—will be gone."

Muttered curses followed this pronouncement.

"And the brides have to be approved by Aunt Cornelia," Justin said.

If the situation hadn't been so surreal, Alex would have laughed. If Cornelia'd had to approve *Harry's* brides, Alex's and his brothers' lives would have been very different.

Harry nodded. "She's a shrewd woman. She'll know if any of the women aren't good wife material."

Alex looked at Gray, whose expression was furious.

Ignoring their incredulity, Harry went on. "You can't tell the women you're rich, nor that you're my sons. I don't want another fortune hunter in the family. God knows, I married enough of them myself. I don't want any of my sons making the same mistakes I made."

That's for sure, Alex thought. Every

single woman Harry had ever married had been a gold digger. And Alex's mother was probably the biggest gold digger of them all. As always, thoughts of his mother produced feelings of bitterness. Alex shook it off. Long ago he'd decided dwelling on the subject of his mother was counter-productive.

"I don't know about my brothers," Justin finally said, "but my answer is that you can take my job and shove it. Nobody tells me who to marry, or if I'll marry, or when I'll have kids."

Harry's expression changed. For a moment, Alex actually thought his father's feelings had been hurt. But hell, what did the old man expect? He was treating them like chattel. As though their feelings didn't matter at all. Did he think they'd just lie down and take it? After all, they *were* his sons. But no one had *ever* told Harry what to do.

"So be it," Harry said, his voice hardening. He looked around. "What about the rest of you?"

Alex nodded. "I'm not my mother. You can't buy me."

Although the brothers all agreed, Harry didn't back down. His last words before leaving them were, "I'll give all of you some time to rethink your positions. You have until 8:00 p.m. Pacific time—three days from now. If I don't hear from you to the contrary before then, I'll tell my lawyers to start looking for a buyer for HuntCom."

"Son-of-a-bitch," Justin swore softly as the door closed behind Harry.

"He's bluffing," Gray said. "He'd never sell the company." His cell phone rang and he glanced at the caller ID before tucking it back in his pocket. "Even if he does hold the controlling interest." Gray was referring to the fact that their father held fifty-one percent of the stock in HuntCom, so even if all four of them plus their Aunt Cornelia voted no to a sale, Harry's wishes would prevail.

"I don't see it happening, either," J.T. said. But there was doubt in his voice.

"I don't know," Justin said slowly. "Cornelia says Harry's been different since his heart attack."

Alex hated to admit it, but he agreed with Justin. Even if Harry hadn't had that heart attack, he was a stubborn man. When he made up his mind about something, it was impossible to sway him.

"Different how?" Gray asked dubiously. His cell phone rang again and he glanced at it impatiently.

"She says he's been moody, a word I found it hard to believe the old man even knows."

"Then maybe he *is* serious," Alex said, frowning.

"We're in the middle of a buy-out." Gray shrugged into his jacket. "There's no way he'd consider selling the company until it's finished and that might be months away. He's bluffing."

"How can you be sure?" Alex asked. "What if you're wrong? Do you want to take that chance? Lose everything you've worked for over the past eighteen years?

I know I sure as hell don't want to see the Hunt Foundation shut down…or run by someone else." For years now, Alex had headed the foundation, the philanthropic arm of HuntCom. For Alex, it was more than a job. It was his passion, his raison d'être. As far as he was concerned, the best thing about being a Hunt was the ability and means to do some good in the world.

The brothers continued to discuss Harry's ultimatum, but since they weren't getting anywhere, they finally decided to call it a night.

"I'll see you at the office tomorrow," Gray said to J.T. as they all moved toward the door. "We need to go over the figures for that possible plant in Singapore."

Alex walked with his brothers down the hallway and out of the house to the parking deck, which was halfway up the hillside overlooking Lake Washington. Every time he came here, he marveled at the beauty of the place. Across the lake, the lights of the Seattle skyline shimmered.

Not that Alex wanted to live in a place like this one. Who the hell needed a mansion, anyway? Even when all four of them had lived with Harry, they'd rattled around in the place. And now that their father was alone except for the servants, it seemed ludicrous to have a place this large. But Harry seemed to need the trappings of wealth.

Alex continued to think about his father's edict as he drove his silver Navigator back to the city where he kept an apartment downtown near the Hunt Foundation offices.

By the time he'd gotten home, fixed himself a drink and a salad and warmed up some leftover chicken piccata that he'd made two days earlier, he was completely convinced that he and his brothers had done the right thing in turning down their father's deal. It was simply too manipulative. Too cold and calculating. Besides, he was now beginning to think, like Gray, that Harry was bluffing.

Sure, he was stubborn, but Alex had a

feeling Harry was counting on the fact his sons knew how stubborn he could be to convince them that he meant what he had said. But Alex also knew his father had worked far too long and too hard to build his empire to ever give it up.

No.

He'd never sell everything. All they had to do was wait him out, and he'd back down.

So when Alex and his brothers were conferenced into a call from Justin the following evening and Justin said he thought they should take the deal, Alex was shocked, even though Justin explained why he thought so.

"I went to see Cornelia," he said. "And she feels there's a strong possibility Harry's threat to sell the company is real. She said she's been growing increasingly worried about him since his heart attack. She confided that Harry seems uncharacteristically introspective and that on several occasions he's told her all he wants is for us to be married and to have children. Cornelia says she's afraid Harry feels a need to right his wrongs and is getting his fiscal and emotional affairs in order in preparation for dying."

"So you're willing to let him choose your *wife?*" Alex said to Justin in disbelief.

"No," Justin said. "I'm willing to convince him that's what's happening, but I'll do the choosing. I spend half my time in Idaho, not Seattle. I'll marry someone acceptable to him and set her up in a home in the city and then I'll go back to Idaho."

"You think that'll work?" The question came from J.T.

"Oh, yeah," Justin drawled, cynicism lacing his tone. "The second she realizes she's married to a Hunt and has a generous allowance, she'll gladly live in Seattle while I live wherever the hell I want. I'll write off the cost of keeping her and the kid as a business expense."

"Damn, Justin," Alex said. "That's cold." Not to mention dishonest. But Alex didn't say that. He knew his brothers all thought he was too idealistic, that he simply didn't understand the cold realities of the world.

"Not cold. Practical," Justin said.

"You know this won't work unless all of us are in," Gray said.

"I know," Justin said. "And it won't work for any of us unless we come up with a contract that ties Harry's hands in the future. We'd have to make sure he can never blackmail us like this again."

"Absolutely," J.T. put in. "If he thinks he can manipulate us with threats, he'll do it again in a heartbeat."

"So if we do this, we are going to need an iron-clad contract that controls the situation," Alex said, thinking out loud.

"If all Harry had threatened us with was loss of income," Justin said, "I'd tell him to go to hell and walk. But I'm not willing to lose the ranch. What about the rest of you?"

Alex finally broke the silence that followed his question. "If it was just money, I'd tell him to go to hell, too. But it's not, is it?"

"It's about the things and places he knows matter most to us." J.T. sounded grim.

"Part of Harry's demand was that the brides not know our identities until after we're married. How are you going to find a marriageable woman in Seattle who doesn't know you're rich, Justin?" Gray asked.

"I've been out of state for most of the last eighteen months, plus I've never been as high-profile as the rest of you," Justin said.

"Yeah, right," J.T. scoffed. "There isn't a single one of us who hasn't had our picture in the paper or a magazine."

"But not as often as Harry," Gray said. "He's the public face of HuntCom. I've got to give the old man credit, he deflected as much publicity from us as he could."

"True," Justin agreed. "So how about it, Gray? Are you in?"

Alex knew Gray could be as stubborn as Harry. "Face it, Gray. Harry holds all the cards."

"He always has." Gray sighed audibly. "This totally sucks, but if we can come up with a way to tie Harry's hands in the future, then I guess I'm in."

By the time they finished their call, Alex was already thinking of ways he could fulfill his part of their strange bargain and begin his own hunt for Cinderella.

*Chapter One*

*Six weeks later...*

Alex looked around his new apartment with satisfaction. This place, with its nondescript decor and discount-house furniture, was a far cry from his pad in the city, but he didn't mind. He didn't need fancy digs. Never had. The only reason he lived where and how he did was because it was expected of him in his position as the director of the Harrison Hunt Foundation.

Thinking about the foundation, he frowned. He'd put out every fire, assigned as many tasks as he could to others and taken care of everything else he could think of before telling his staff he was taking an extended leave of absence. And he knew his assistant, Martha Oliver, affectionately called Marti by all who knew her well, could be trusted to handle ninety-nine percent of anything else that might come up.

But it was that other one percent that worried Alex. Still, he was only a ninety-minute drive from downtown Seattle, and in an emergency, Marti could reach him on his cell and know he'd come as soon as possible. In fact, she'd been texting him religiously, keeping him up to date on everything. Alex made a mental note to give her a hefty bonus when this situation was finally resolved and he was back to work. Which, he hoped, would be soon.

He knew there was no reason to worry. Things would be fine while he was gone. He reminded himself that all he had to do was quickly find a suitable woman to marry, and he might not have to be away from the foundation for long at all.

Alex was not arrogant or vain. But he wasn't unaware of his appeal. All his life he'd been told he was good-looking and wherever he went women made eye contact and flirted. So if he found someone who interested him and that he felt his father and his Aunt Cornelia would approve of, he suspected all he'd have to do was go through the motions women expected from a suitor.

After he and his brothers had decided to go along with Harry's edict, Alex had given considerable thought to his strategy in the campaign to find the kind of wife he wanted. What he'd decided was he would never be able to do so while continuing to work at the foundation. He needed to go somewhere he wasn't known and he needed to be working at an ordinary job with ordinary people.

Then he thoroughly researched Harry's various holdings and narrowed them down to the one where he thought he might not stick out like a sore thumb. He told his father he wanted a position at their distribution center in Jansen, an hour and a half drive from Seattle—just south of Olympia. He already knew most folks in Jansen watched Portland television stations and read the Portland newspaper, so they'd be unlikely to recognize him from any of the publicity photos tied to the Hunt Foundation. And if anyone *did* recognize him, he'd simply say he was always being mistaken for one of the Hunt brothers.

Alex didn't think he had to worry. He had always tried to keep a low profile. He hated society bashes and disliked the club scene. If not for the foundation and its work, he doubted anyone would ever recognize him as belonging to the Hunt family.

Today would be the true test, though, because in less than forty-five minutes, he would begin his new job at HuntCom's main distribution center.

New job.

New apartment.

And new name.

He'd also decided that for the duration of his "hunt" he would be known as Alex Noble. It would be different if he were going to go to work somewhere that wasn't associated with HuntCom, but at the distribution center there was no way he could be Alex Hunt without someone questioning the coincidence of the shared name.

So he'd decided on Noble, which was the surname of a previous stepfather. Alex's mother, Lucinda Parker Hunt Noble Fitzpatrick, was on her third marriage and Alex had once cynically figured it wouldn't be her last, although he'd finally conceded that maybe Terrence Fitzpatrick was the real deal. He and Alex's mother had recently celebrated their twenty-fourth wedding anniversary.

There were things about Terrence Alex didn't like, namely his penchant for thinking money could solve any problem, but he'd done one thing right. He'd given Alex a much-loved younger sister, Julie, although Terrence was doing his level best to spoil her with the enormous amounts of money and gifts he lavished upon her.

Thinking about Julie and her recent escapades, Alex frowned. He wished he could get through to her, but she laughed off his concern, telling him he was "stodgy" and "old-fashioned" and had forgotten what it was like to be young.

Her scorn, even though delivered with affection, had hurt. Alex didn't think he was stodgy. He was just sensible and practical. So he didn't worship at the altar of money and power. Did that mean there was something wrong with him? He guessed in his little sister's crowd, it probably did.

He was still thinking about Julie when he pulled into the employee parking lot at the HuntCom Distribution Center. But when he emptied his pockets and passed through security, he deliberately put her out of his mind. Today he couldn't afford to be distracted by Julie or anything else. He would need all his wits about him to pull off a successful masquerade.

It took an hour to fill out necessary paperwork and watch an orientation film in the human resources department, but by nine o'clock—he was on the first shift which began at eight in the morning—the HR manager's assistant, who made a point of telling him her name was Kim, walked him down to the gigantic storage center, which was a beehive of activity.

Alex couldn't help grinning when a young girl with purple spiked hair whizzed by them on roller blades. At his quizzical look, Kim said, "That's Ruby. She's also a picker."

Alex frowned. "Picker?"

"Sorry. Merchandise rep. Same job you're going to do. You know, *pick* the merchandise from the shelves so it can be shipped to the company or person who placed the order."

"Ah." It amused Alex to think what his colleagues at the foundation would say if they could see him now. Most, he knew, were in awe of him. After all, he was one of the mighty Hunts. They respected him, because he worked as hard or harder than they did, and they knew he cared about the work they were doing, but they still couldn't manage to treat him the way they treated the others on staff. To them, he was out of their league.

"I'm sure you'll be great at the job," Kim said, giving him an admiring glance.

Alex wasn't interested; he'd seen her wedding band. So all he said was, "Hope so."

She led Alex toward a cluster of several people who seemed to be arguing about something. When they spied him, the conversation abruptly stopped and a young woman—a very *attractive* young woman, Alex noticed—with wildly curly red hair tied back with a navy-blue ribbon and dressed in snug jeans and a white blouse open at the throat, broke away from the group and strode toward them. Very blue eyes filled with intelligence gave him a quick assessment before turning their intensity on Kim.

"Um, P.J.," she said, "this is Alex Noble,

the new member of your crew. Alex, this is P.J. Kincaid, the floor supervisor."

Alex wondered if P.J. had adopted initials in lieu of her first name for the same reason J.T. had adopted his, because she hated her given name. J.T. had said Jared was a sissy name and he would kill anyone who insisted upon using it.

"Hello," P.J. said, thrusting out her right hand. "Welcome to HuntCom."

Alex took her hand and gave it a firm shake. Hers was just as firm. "Hello," he said.

"Good luck," Kim said. She smiled at him, then turned and walked off.

When Alex's attention returned to P.J., her eyes met his squarely. Something about their steady scrutiny disturbed Alex. Did she suspect something? He forced himself not to drop his gaze.

"I'm told you have experience," she said.

Yes, that was definitely a hint of doubt in her voice. Deciding brevity was his best bet, Alex nodded. "Yes, I do."

"And you worked…*where*…before?"

Sticking to what it said on his fake résumé, Alex answered, "At a warehouse in Sacramento."

She looked at him thoughtfully. "What kind of products?"

"Household appliances."

Her eyes remained speculative. "Why'd you leave?"

He made his voice light. "Couldn't very well commute from here."

She nodded, but instinct told him she wasn't completely buying his story. "You've completed all your paperwork?"

"Yes."

"Had your physical and drug testing?"

"Yes." That wasn't true, but on paper, it said Alex had done so and passed.

"So…you ready to go to work?"

"Yes, I am."

Turning, she gestured to one of the men in the group still gathered nearby. "Rick."

A dark-haired, dark-eyed man Alex judged to be in his late twenties or early thirties walked toward them. Like P.J. and

Alex and almost everyone Alex had seen so far, except for the employees of the HR department, he wore jeans. His black T-shirt hawked a Red Hot Chili Peppers concert.

"Rick," she said, "this is Alex Noble. You'll be training him." Meeting Alex's eyes again, she said, "Alex, this is Rick Alvarado. He's been with the company seven years and can answer any questions you might have."

The two men shook hands. Rick's eyes were friendly. Alex liked him immediately and sensed he could turn out to be a friend.

"Follow me," Rick said. "I'll give you a tour of the place so you can get a general idea of where everything is stored." He kept up a running commentary as they headed down the nearest aisle. "You know much about the company, Alex?"

Alex nodded. "Quite a bit. I researched it when I knew I was going to be working here."

"So you know old man Hunt started out

by coming up with a new software and things escalated from there?"

Alex nodded.

"Now we manufacture just about everything in the computer field," Rick continued. "We have over three thousand products that we ship from this location."

"That many?" Alex said, although he'd already known this.

"Keeps us hopping 24/7. We run three shifts. Eight to four, four to twelve, twelve to eight. Lots of the guys like the afternoon and night shifts, but me, I like days. 'Course, I work the other shifts anytime they need extra hands, 'cause it's overtime, and with three little girls and a wife who likes to give those old charge cards a workout..." He laughed. "I can always use the money."

"Three little girls, huh?"

Rick grinned. "Yeah, we had 'em pretty close together. My oldest is eight, the youngest is four." Pulling a wallet from his hip pocket, he took out several photos. "I'll only do this once," he promised, handing Alex the pictures.

Alex smiled at the likenesses. All three girls had curly dark hair and dark eyes. "They sure are cute."

"Yeah," Rick said proudly. "They're good kids, too. Maria, she's been a stay-at-home mom, but in September Jenny, she's the youngest, starts school, so Maria's going to go back to work."

"What does she do?" Alex asked politely.

"She's a preschool teacher. She'll be teaching at Jenny's school."

By now, they'd stopped in a densely stocked aisle.

"You don't have to remember everything I'm gonna show you," Rick said. "I'm just giving you an overview. You'll get a diagram of the place and a product list showing where each of the different products can be found. It'll take you a while, but after a couple of weeks, you'll be an old pro at this."

Alex hoped so. The last thing he wanted to do was fuel that doubt he'd seen in his new boss's eyes. He was going to have a hard enough time of it remembering to keep in character without worrying about keeping *her* happy, too. "This place is huge. Do we fill orders from all over or just in certain areas?"

"The center's divided into four quadrants," Rick said. "Our unit fills orders for Quad B. I'll show you. We'll walk the whole quad. Actually, you'll probably want to become familiar with all the quads eventually."

"Why is that?"

"Sometimes certain products sell heavily, like when we're running a special promotion or something, and you might be asked to fill in at one of the other quads."

Alex nodded. That made sense. "Does P.J. supervise all the quads?"

Rick nodded. "Yep. She's the boss. Only one higher than her here is Steve Mallery, the GM."

Just then, the girl with the purple hair skated by.

"Ruby," Alex said.

Rick laughed. "You know about her, huh?"

"The clerk who brought me down from HR told me her name."

"Ruby looks like a punk rocker with those tattoos and all the body piercings, but she's okay. She's one of our best pickers."

"I admit I was surprised to see the roller blades."

"A couple of the kids use them. Wish I could skate. I'd wear 'em, too. You can sure get around faster. But I'd probably kill myself. Or if not that, break a leg or something."

"I know what you mean," Alex said, although he prided himself on being physically fit. Still, he wasn't a skater. Never had been.

Rick smiled and turned his attention back to the merchandise. "Okay, Alex, lesson number one. Here's how we stock the products...."

Frat boy.

It was the first thing P.J. thought when

she was introduced to Alex. What was *he* doing there? All P.J.'d had to do was look at him to know he didn't belong. He was too good-looking and way too polished. His hands alone told the story. No calluses. No rough skin. Clean, manicured nails. Long, elegant fingers.

And then there were his teeth. P.J. always noticed people's teeth, for they indicated class and financial status more than anything else. And Alex's teeth were gorgeous—straight and white. Obviously, they'd been well cared for.

She wondered if he'd once held a top-level job, maybe lost it due to drugs or alcohol. *Or maybe he's a corporate spy, sent here to find out if we're doing a good job. If I'm doing a good job.*

The thought was sobering. It also pissed her off. Because P.J. worked hard, harder even than her crew. She had to. She was a woman supervising mostly men. She constantly had to prove herself.

Geez, if corporate wanted to know what was going on here, all they had to do was talk to Steve, or better yet, be above board and come and observe the center openly. They'd soon see what a tight ship she ran.

Well, she'd keep a close eye on Alex Noble. And if he *was* a spy, she'd soon find out. In the meantime, she wouldn't trust him as far as she could throw him. And yet, even as she was telling herself all of this, she couldn't deny the frisson of attraction she'd felt when they shook hands. Acknowledging this, she was infuriated with her body's betrayal.

*What's wrong with you?* Alex Noble was so not the kind of man she wanted in her life. Ever since she was old enough to know better, she'd envisioned herself with a man who held the same beliefs she did: say, a union boss or champion of migrant workers. Someone she could respect and admire for his ideas and not how well he filled out a pair of jeans.

Certainly not for his sexy dimples or his thick, wavy hair or his dark-chocolate eyes.

*Dark chocolate!*

Had she *really* thought that?

But even as she chastised herself for the gushy term, she knew it applied. His eyes really had reminded her of dark chocolate. Sweet, melt-in-your-mouth dark chocolate. The kind of eyes a woman could lose herself in. Just remembering the way he'd looked at her gave her a funny feeling in her stomach.

*Oh, man, Kincaid, you've been celibate way too long. You really need to get laid.*

"P.J."

P.J. jumped.

"You looked like you were miles away. I called your name twice."

The speaker was P.J.'s best friend at work—Anna Garcia. Actually, for the past six years, Anna had been P.J.'s best friend, period. P.J. smiled at the pretty brunette. "What's up?"

"We having lunch together today?"

"Sure."

"Great. Want to eat in the cafeteria or outside?"

"It's a nice day. Let's eat outside." When

the distribution center had been built, HuntCom had made sure the area surrounding was beautifully landscaped and that there were pockets of trees and flower beds interspersed with walkways and areas with picnic tables. Employees were urged to use the grounds on their breaks, although the smokers grumbled that there were too few places for them to indulge in their habit. Although P.J. didn't admire many corporate titans—she'd grown up around too many of them—Harrison Hunt actually seemed to care about his employees.

*Be fair. So does Dad.*

Well, yes, her own father also treated his employees fairly and sometimes even generously. But he and Harrison Hunt seemed to be the exceptions.

After Anna had headed back to the mailing center, which she supervised, P.J. printed out the newest batch of orders that had come through in the past hour. After sorting them, she handed the orders for Quads A, C, and D to Chick Fogarty, her assistant, to distribute, then walked toward aisle 24, where they stocked some of the peripherals in their inventory. She knew this was where Rick would have started Alex's training.

Sure enough, the two men were standing in front of the section where the eighteen different mouses they sold were stored, and although P.J. stood well back as she watched, she could hear Rick naming them as he pointed out how they were arranged by model number.

"I can't believe there are so many different kinds," Alex was saying. "Do we really sell all of them?"

"Yeah, we do," Rick answered. "Hey, I personally have three at home. A wireless, a basic USB plug-in, and a mini for when I travel. You got a computer?"

Alex nodded. "Yeah. I bought myself a laptop last year."

"One of ours?"

"Uh, no. I guess I shouldn't say that too loud."

"Not if you don't want the boss lady to

hear." Rick glanced over at P.J. and grinned. "'Course, it's too late. She already did."

Alex whipped around.

P.J. almost laughed at the guilty expression on his face. Walking over to them, she said, "It's okay, Alex. Buying a Hunt computer is not a prerequisite for working here. However, we do give a hefty discount to our employees, so if you decide to upgrade or buy something else in our product line, you'll save quite a bit of money."

Deciding Rick had everything under control, P.J. handed him half the stack of new orders. "You can get started on these whenever you feel Alex is ready."

Rick gave her a salute. "Okay, boss."

Alex's eyes met hers briefly before he looked away. And once again, P.J. felt that unwelcome spark of awareness and attraction.

She frowned. Damn. She had to get control of herself and quit acting like a silly teenager.

Quickly striding away, she decided the

best thing for her would be to give Alex Noble a wide berth. A really wide berth. On the other hand, that wouldn't be the best thing for HuntCom.

In fact, she should probably keep a close eye on him these first few weeks. Make sure he was actually doing the job he'd been hired to do.

But for the rest of the morning, she kept her distance. She would quiz Rick later, see what he thought. Maybe she was just paranoid about Alex because he was so attractive. Face it, she chided herself, you've been exposed to too many good-looking, self-centered, arrogant men in your lifetime and now you think they're *all* like that.

Maybe Alex Noble would prove to be the exception.

Yeah, right.

But P.J. wasn't going to hold her breath.

## Chapter Two

"I thought there was a hiring freeze."

P.J. made a face. "Yeah. That's what I thought, too." She and Anna were just finishing up lunch.

Anna popped the last bite of her tunafish sandwich into her mouth, then wiped her mouth with her napkin. "But Jimmy said you've got a new picker."

P.J. nodded.

"So what's the deal?"

"You tell me."

"Me?" Anna laughed. "You're kidding, right?"

"Well, you usually hear all the gossip, so I thought if anyone would know what's going on, you would," P.J. pointed out. That was the other thing about Alex Noble—maybe even the most important thing—the fact he'd been foisted on her without any warning.

"I haven't heard a word," Anna said. "Not a peep." She reached for a plastic bag filled with cut-up apple.

P.J. polished off her turkey sandwich, accompanied by a handful of potato chips—she was a junk-food addict, much to her mother's chagrin. "Not even from Ben?" Ben Garza was the HR Director and he'd had a thing for Anna for a while.

Anna made a face. "I've been avoiding Ben."

P.J. refrained from saying something trite like *you could do worse*. She knew how sick she was of people trying to pair her off with guys who didn't interest her in the slightest. Still, she almost felt sorry for Ben. He wasn't the best-looking guy in the world, but he had a good job and he seemed really decent. But Anna simply wasn't interested. She'd gone out with him twice and told P.J. that the thought of going to bed with him actually turned her stomach.

"So what's he like?"

"The new guy?"

Anna laughed. "Yes, P.J., the new guy."

P.J. frowned and finished chewing and swallowing before answering. "I don't know. He doesn't seem to belong here."

"What do you mean?"

"He's too good-looking. Too…sophisticated or something."

Anna chewed thoughtfully on a piece of apple. "Tina said he's a hunk."

"Tina? When did *she* see him?"

"She snuck down to your area earlier this morning. Said she wanted to check him out." Anna grinned. "We don't get that many eligible guys here. *Handsome* eligible guys. Every woman in the place is going to be checking him out. Maybe they already have." Anna's grin turned sly. "So if you want him, P.J., you'd better stake your claim early."

"*Want* him? I have absolutely no interest in Alex Noble. Believe me, he's not my type."

"What's wrong with him?"

"I told you. He's too good-looking." The truth was, Alex looked like he belonged in her sisters' crowd. The country club, golf and tennis crowd. The Armani crowd. The kind of men P.J. had wanted to get away from.

"Tina says he looks like Colin Firth."

"Who the hell is Colin Firth?" Irritation made P.J.'s voice increase in volume.

Anna looked at her as if she'd suddenly grown two heads. "You mean there's a female alive on this earth who doesn't know Colin Firth?" Her voice was laced with astonishment.

"What is he? A movie star? You know I don't pay attention to those people." In P.J.'s opinion, movie stars were only a cut above rock stars, and P.J. considered them the armpit of the universe, with no re-deeming social value whatsoever.

Anna sighed. "Honey, Colin Firth is way more than a movie star. He's the most gorgeous guy to come along in years. He's British and has one of those upper-crust accents that is sooo sexy. He also has dreamy dark eyes, he's tall, and he lives in a villa in Tuscany." She sighed again. "Un-fortunately, he's married."

P.J. rolled her eyes. Honestly, even sensible Anna could be an airhead at times. "Alex Noble isn't *that* good-looking."

"No? Well, with your ideas about men, I don't think I can trust your judgment, P.J. I think I'll have to have a look myself."

P.J. abruptly stood and began clearing up her trash. "Oh, for God's sake. Come and drool all over him. I certainly don't care. Just make sure you don't distract him from his work."

"Somebody certainly is testy all of a sudden," Anna said, giving P.J. a knowing look.

P.J. knew she'd overreacted, and for the

life of her, she didn't know why. All she knew was, she was heartily sick of the subject of Alex Noble.

Alex was beat.

He'd thought he was in great physical shape. Hell, he worked out three times a week at the gym and played tennis at least three times a week. But he had a soft job at the foundation, mainly sitting on his butt. And today, for the first time since he'd spent a summer building houses with Habitat for Humanity, he'd done physical labor, with lots of stretching, kneeling and lifting. He'd used muscles he hadn't even known he had. So by the time four o'clock rolled around, he was more than ready to leave.

Other than that, he was satisfied with how the day had gone. He found it interesting seeing how many orders came through during his shift and how much work was involved in filling them and getting the merchandise shipped out. Although before he started this job, he'd studied the numbers associated with HuntCom and its myriad arms, actually seeing all the products they manufactured and sold was a real eye-opener.

Whether you worshiped at the altar of money and power or not, you had to admire what Harry had accomplished. It wasn't as if he'd come from money. Just the opposite, in fact. Alex's Hunt grandparents had been squarely middle-class. His grandfather Hunt owned a small hardware store; his grandmother had been a stay-at-home mom.

And Harry had been a too-tall, just-this-side-of-weird, geek.

Yet look what he'd accomplished. He'd developed ground-breaking software that had changed the personal computer industry practically overnight and followed that by designing cutting edge hardware that was as good as or better than anything else on the market.

Now he was worth billions.

And he employed thousands of people.

Alex had met a couple of dozen of those

people today. Among them several attractive women. Two of those women seemed promising as far as his bride hunt went— one worked in the mail room, one was a picker from a different quad—although he'd have to know more about both of them before he could make any kind of decision. After all, he was talking about the future mother of his children.

Too bad P.J. Kincaid didn't have a more agreeable personality, because she was definitely the most intriguing of the women he'd met. But she hadn't even made his short list. He didn't have time to win over someone who obviously didn't like him.

She'd certainly made no secret of her feelings. In fact, as the day wore on, she'd seemed to be more suspicious of him rather than less, even though he'd worked hard and given her no cause to look at him the way she had.

What was her problem, anyway?

Why did she seem to always be watching him?

Alex knew she'd asked Rick about him,

because he'd seen the two of them talking and Rick kept glancing Alex's way the whole time. In some ways, this amused Alex, because Rick was obviously not the cloak-and-dagger type. In other ways, it didn't amuse Alex at all.

Alex didn't think P.J. could possibly know who he was or why he was there, so why was she acting so weird? Was it because *she* hadn't hired him? Did she resent the fact he'd been presented to her as a fait accompli? Alex grimaced. He'd bet that was it. She felt he'd been pushed on her. Well, in that case, maybe he could change her mind about him.

Question was, did he want to?

The minute P.J. closed her apartment door behind her, she began stripping off her clothes. Today more than any other, she felt the need to get outside and work the kinks out. She could hardly wait to put on her running clothes and shoes and hit the park.

A scant ten minutes later, she was in her

bright-blue Miata convertible—top down, breeze ruffling her hair—and heading for the Jansen River and the park that had been built along its banks. Washington State looked beautiful in late summer, she thought, with its riot of colorful flowers and lush green lawns. People complained about all the rain they got, but without the rain, the landscape would be as brown as California's. As she drove along, idly enjoying the scenery, her mind once again drifted to her new employee.

Just as Anna had predicted, throughout the afternoon, at least half a dozen women from different departments at the distribution center had come, on the flimsiest of excuses, to check out Alex Noble.

One of them, Carrie Wancheck, a twenty-one-year-old who worked in payroll, hadn't even bothered with an excuse. She'd grinned at P.J., saying in a stage whisper, "I just wanted to see the hunk everyone's talking about."

"He's too old for you," P.J. had snapped.

Carrie's smile was knowing. "I like

older men. They're usually the best lovers."

P.J. had had to force herself not to say anything else, because she realized it might sound as if she were jealous or something. Jealous! Nothing could be farther from the truth. She had absolutely *no* interest in Alex Noble. None. Zero. Nada. But she knew how the women at the center could be. If you said you weren't interested in someone, they immediately thought you were lying. Especially when the man in question was as attractive as Alex Noble.

So she'd kept quiet and silently fumed instead. *Dammit.* She needed this kind of distraction in her department like she needed a hole in the head. If they were going to palm off a new employee, the least they could have done was make him homely.

And the women in her own department were the worst of all! Even Ruby, who was only nineteen and a year out of high school, had hung around Alex to the point where P.J. had to say something to her. P.J. had wanted to add that she didn't think a man like Alex would be interested in a kid with purple spiked hair, five earrings on each ear, and a rose tattoo down her right arm, but despite her appearance, Ruby was a nice kid, and P.J. liked her, so she just sighed and told Ruby to get back to work, then watched the girl skate away.

She was so engrossed in thinking about Alex Noble and the disruption he'd caused today that she almost passed up the entrance to the park.

Hitting the brakes, she managed to slow down in time to turn onto the driveway. Five minutes later, settled into a nice easy jogging rhythm, she finally managed to put Alex Noble and the rest of the irritations of the day out of her mind.

Just as he had taken off his clothes and was heading into the shower, Alex's cell phone rang. He thought about ignoring it, then sighed, reached for it and looked at the caller ID. It was his sister Julie.

"Hey," he said. "I hope this doesn't mean you're in trouble again."

"Hey, yourself," Julie said, her voice filled with amusement. "Why would you assume I'm in trouble? Can't I just call to say hello?"

"Yes, but you rarely do."

"Now Alex…is that nice?"

Alex chuckled. Deciding this call might take awhile, he grabbed a towel from the towel rack and, tucking the phone under his chin, wrapped the towel around himself, then sat on the rim of the tub to continue the conversation. "So if you're not in trouble, what's up, Jules?"

"I called to invite you to my birthday bash."

"That's right. You *have* got a birthday coming up soon."

"Don't pretend you forgot."

Alex smiled. They both knew he never forgot her birthday. In fact, he'd already bought her gift—earrings and a matching bracelet designed by a local artist who worked in silver and semi-precious stones.

The moment Alex had spied the pair set with deep-blue tourmalines, he'd known they were perfect for his sister, whose eyes were an exact match. "So where's the party going to be?"

"Well, believe it or not, it's going to be at the house."

"That's certainly different." Usually Julie's parties took place at one of the many clubs she and her friends frequented.

"Mom insisted."

"And bribed you how?"

Julie laughed. "I want a new car."

"A new car?" Alex said in disbelief. "Your Mini Cooper is only two years old."

"I know, but I'm tired of it."

Alex mentally shook his head. He remembered how Julie had wheedled when she'd wanted that car. "So what do you want now?"

"I saw this really gorgeous black Lotus—"

"Lotus! Geez, Jules, you're talking, what, sixty thousand or more?"

"Daddy can afford it."

"That's not the point. You don't need a car like that."

"Need has nothing to do with it."

Alex sighed. She was so damn spoiled. There was no doubt in his mind that his stepfather would buy her the Lotus.

"Anyway, will you come to my party?"

"When is it?"

"On my birthday. It's a Friday, so that works out great. Seven o'clock. You can bring a date, too, if you want."

"No date."

"But *you'll* be there, right?"

"I'll be there."

"Mom'll be happy."

Alex grunted. His mother had been attempting for a long time to get back into his good graces, but no matter how she tried to make it up to him, Alex found it almost impossible to forget that when he was only two years old, she'd given custody of him to Harry.

Hell, every single one of Harry's wives had sold out for money. Although he and his half-brothers rarely talked about it, Alex couldn't help but think Justin, J.T. and Gray had been just as affected by their mothers' abandonment as Alex had. Because what else could you call it when your mother took money in exchange for giving sole custody of you to your father?

At least Alex, as the next to youngest, had only had to get used to one stepmother—Justin's mother—and she hadn't lasted all that long. Gray, on the other hand, had gone through three stepmothers, all of whom had a short shelf life with Harry. No wonder Gray was so mistrustful of women.

It was pretty sad, but the only stable female influence in their lives was their Aunt Cornelia. And she wasn't technically their aunt at all, even though they'd referred to her that way all their lives. She was actually the widow of Harry's best friend, and it was Alex's private belief that Harry had been in love with Cornelia for years.

As Julie continued to chatter excitedly

about the car she coveted, Alex wondered if it would do any good for him to talk to his stepfather about her. Alex didn't want his sister to turn out like their mother, and indulging her the way her father did wouldn't encourage her to be any different.

But as much as he wanted to do something, he knew he'd better not. Terrence would get his hackles up if Alex said anything to him. No sense causing any more tension in the family.

When Julie wound down, they said their goodbyes—Julie exacting one more promise from Alex that he'd be at her party—and Alex tossed the towel he'd been wearing onto the towel rack. He started to step into the tub when he suddenly changed his mind. Even though he was tired, he knew he'd feel better if he got some *real* exercise today. Something to unkink his muscles and blow the stink off. After that he could come home and shower and crash with a beer and dinner.

Twenty minutes later, dressed in shorts,

a Coldplay T-shirt Julie had given him along with their newest CD, and his cross-trainers, he pulled into Jansen Park. Although running wasn't his favorite activity, in the absence of a tennis partner, it would do. He still hadn't found a gym to join, but he hoped to remedy that soon, too.

He was about halfway through his run when one of the runners coming toward him from the opposite direction looked familiar to him. As she got closer, he realized it was his boss, the prickly P.J. Kincaid.

Well, well.

His gaze took in the riot of red hair inadequately held back by a sweatband, her perspiration-soaked white T-shirt that had molded to her rounded breasts, the navy-blue running shorts that showed off her nice firm butt, and her long, shapely legs with their well-defined calf muscles. Prickly or not, she sure was easy on the eyes.

He knew the exact moment when she

realized who he was. Her eyes widened, her nice, even rhythm faltered, and she nearly stumbled.

Recovering quickly, she stopped, and when her breathing had slowed enough to speak, she said, "Hello, Alex."

"Hi." Alex mopped his brow with the towel he'd thrown around his neck.

"So you're a runner, are you?"

Damn, those blue eyes of hers were unnerving. "Not much of one, I'm afraid."

She shrugged. "You're here."

"I need the exercise. You run here a lot?"

"Every day."

No wonder she looked as good as she did. "How far does this trail go?" he asked to distract himself from just how good she looked.

"If you go all the way around, it's exactly five miles." Now her gaze held a challenge. "You plan to do the whole trail?"

"I thought I would," he said, although he hadn't planned anything of the kind.

"Good." She looked at her black sports watch. "Well, I'd better get going. I'm meeting my sister for dinner at seven and if I don't hurry, I'll be late." She gave him a wave as she set off. "See you tomorrow."

Alex couldn't help it.

Instead of continuing on his way immediately, he watched her. Yes, she certainly did have a nice butt. In fact, it was one of the nicest butts he'd seen in a long time. It would fit very nicely in a man's hands.

And those legs!

Alex couldn't stop himself from imagining those legs twined around a man when making love.

It was at that moment Alex decided maybe he'd forget about playing tennis and joining a gym. Maybe running here in the evenings was a much more sensible choice.

## Chapter Three

P.J. wanted to turn around and look back in the worst way. Yet the last thing, the very last thing she wanted was for Alex Noble to think she was interested in him like the rest of those silly women at work.

Because she wasn't.

Not at all.

But, she thought grudgingly, she had to admit he was good to look at. Idly, she wondered how tall he was. At least six-two or six-three, she imagined. P.J. had always had a thing for tall men. Maybe that was because at five-seven she was on the tall side herself. And the rare times she got dressed up, she liked wearing three-inch heels. She also liked looking up when she was with a man. No Katie Holmes–Tom Cruise thing for her!

*Will you stop it? Alex Noble is not in the running as an escort or anything else. Remember that. He's an employee. Your employee. So even if you were interested— and you're not!—you don't date employees.*

*Ever.*

Yet no matter how many times she told herself to stop thinking about Alex, she couldn't seem to wipe the image of him in those shorts and that T-shirt that defined his well-developed pecs out of her mind.

She thought about him all the way back to her condo. She thought about him as she took a quick shower. She thought about him as she dressed to meet Courtney. And she was still thinking about him as she walked into Mackey's Bar and

Grill in beautiful downtown Webber—which was halfway between Seattle proper and Jansen—at exactly one minute to seven.

Courtney was already there and had secured a booth. She grinned at P.J. and stood to give her a hug. Courtney had inherited their mother's blond hair and green eyes, whereas P.J.'s coloring came from her Grandmother Kincaid. As always, Courtney looked bandbox perfect in creamy linen cropped pants, a short-sleeved black silk summer sweater, and black espadrilles. P.J. couldn't help but notice the beautifully manicured toenails and fingernails sporting a summery shade of coral. In contrast, P.J.'s own nails were unpolished and desperately needed work. And her jeans and T-shirt weren't exactly the latest fashion, either.

*That's what happens when there's no man in your life,* an insidious little voice said. *You forget to pay attention to yourself.* She couldn't even use the excuse of her job, because most of the women at the center paid a lot more attention to their appearance than P.J. did.

She and Courtney had barely said their hellos and how-are-yous when their waiter approached. "What can I get you to drink?" he asked, looking at P.J.

"What have you got on draft?" she asked.

He named the brands.

"No Black Sheep?" P.J. had a weakness for good English ale.

"No, sorry."

"Okay. I'll have a Guinness." She smiled at her sister after he'd left to fill her order. "What're you drinking?"

Courtney made a face. "Ginger ale."

Thinking her sister wasn't having a beer because she had a fairly long drive back to Mercer Island where she and her husband had bought a new home the year before, P.J. said, "One beer should be okay. I mean, you're going to eat before you get behind the wheel again."

Courtney hesitated, her gaze sliding away briefly before returning to meet

P.J.'s. "That's not why I'm not drinking," she finally said.

"Well, what then—?" P.J. stopped abruptly. She fought against feelings she'd thought she'd conquered long ago. Yet here they were again, still hurtful, still unworthy of her, especially considering how much she loved Courtney. "You're pregnant again?" she asked softly.

Courtney nodded. "Three months."

"Three *months!* And you've kept it a secret this long?" P.J. was proud of herself. She sounded just the way she wanted to sound—happy for Courtney and nothing else.

"I wanted to wait till I'd passed the first trimester." Courtney's eyes searched P.J.'s. P.J. knew Courtney was worried about how her news would affect P.J.

Reaching across the table, she took Courtney's hand. "Are you happy about this?" Courtney and her husband already had three kids—a boy, ten, and two little girls, seven and four.

Courtney nodded. "I am. Brad…well, he wants another boy in the worst way."

P.J. refrained from rolling her eyes or saying what she thought about Brad and his *wants*. In her opinion, her sister's husband was a neanderthal. P.J. wouldn't have put up with him for a minute, let alone the twelve years Courtney'd been married to him. For one thing, he didn't believe in women holding jobs outside the home.

For another, he was constantly saying things like, "Honey, you wouldn't understand that even if I *did* explain it," when Courtney asked him about anything to do with his job. You'd think he was a rocket scientist, for God's sake, when he was a lawyer.

Courtney was every bit as smart as he was, probably smarter, P.J. thought. Yet she seemed contented with Brad. His putdowns didn't seem to bother her at all. In fact, she didn't even seem to notice them.

To each his own, P.J. thought. Better her than me.

"Well, if you're happy, then I'm happy for you," she said now. "Congratulations."

"Thanks." Courtney sipped at her ginger ale and eyed her sister over the rim of her glass.

P.J. knew she wanted to say something. To prevent yet another conversation about P.J.'s situation, she hurriedly asked, "Do Mom and Dad know?"

"Not yet."

"You mean, you're telling *me* before you told them?"

"You're my favorite sister, you know that."

They smiled at each other, and P.J. forced herself to remember how lucky she was. She might not ever be able to have any children of her own, and she might have repudiated her family's money and her status as an heiress, but that didn't mean she didn't love her parents and siblings. And she absolutely adored her nieces and nephews—Courtney's three and soon to be four, Jillian's two, and Peter's two.

P.J. told herself it didn't matter if she couldn't have kids, because she had no intention of getting married, anyway. She'd known long ago she wasn't cut out for marriage. In fact, she couldn't imagine subjugating herself to a man…*any* man. Just the idea of a man telling her what she could and couldn't do set her teeth on edge.

And she certainly wasn't cut out for homemaking. Hell, she couldn't even boil water, let alone cook. And as far as cleaning went, forget that, too. One of her indulgences was a once-a-week maid service, and even if she had to give up food, she intended to keep that.

Well, maybe that was an exaggeration. She liked food too much, especially carbs. In fact, she'd never met a carb she didn't like. That was the biggest reason she forced herself to run five miles every day. So she could keep eating all those fries and pasta and pizza and still keep her figure.

Yet, even as she told herself all of this,

she knew she might have been willing to give the marriage thing a try if not for her probable inability to have children. Providing, of course, the right man should come along.

*You can always adopt.*

Maybe, she thought. But there again, it would take the right kind of man. And lately, she'd begun to think he didn't exist.

*Plenty of single women adopt.*

P.J. had actually considered adoption. In fact, she'd given some serious consideration to adopting an older child—one of the ones considered hard to place since everyone seemed to want babies. And maybe one of these days she'd finally get around to doing something about it.

By now the waiter had brought P.J.'s beer and the sisters had placed their orders—P.J. a steak sandwich and fries, Courtney the house specialty of coconut-crusted shrimp salad.

"P.J., you eat entirely too much junk food," Courtney said mildly as their waiter walked off.

"I know. That's why I run."

"Do you ever eat a salad?"

"Sure."

"How often, once a month?"

P.J. grinned. "You know me too well." After taking a swallow of her beer, she said, "So you're due in…mid-February?"

Courtney nodded. "February fourteenth, to be exact."

"At least it's not Christmas day." P.J.'s birthday was two days before Christmas and she'd always hated that. "Just don't name him Valentino or something like that."

Courtney snorted. "Like Brad would let me."

To keep from saying something snide about Brad, P.J. said, "So what else is new?"

"Let's see. Um, Melissa McKee is getting a divorce."

"You're not serious!"

"Melissa's the one who told me."

"That's a shame. I thought she and Rod had a good marriage."

"Hey, he'll be eligible now…" Courtney's eyes were speculative.

P.J. knew what she was thinking. "Forget that," she said quickly. "He's not my type. But he'll have no shortage of women lining up to be the next Mrs. McKee, I'm sure of that."

Rod was a very wealthy man as well as a good-looking one. P.J. wasn't sure what he did. Something in commodities trading, she thought. He probably had no social conscience to speak of. Definitely not her type.

Thinking that, she couldn't help remembering she'd said the same thing about Alex Noble just today, that he was not her type, either. Something in her expression must have alerted Courtney to the direction of her thoughts because her sister said, "Wait a minute. Are you dating someone?"

"What makes you ask that?"

"You had a strange look on your face."

"Oh, I was just thinking about a new guy who started working for me today.

Anna—you've heard me talk about her—said something about him and I told her he wasn't my type, either."

"Why'd she say something about him?"

P.J. shrugged. "He's kind of a hunk. If you like that type."

"And what type is that?"

"Oh, you know, tall, dark, handsome." P.J. smiled in spite of herself.

"And you don't like that type." Courtney shook her head, laughing. "You're one of a kind, you know that?"

Just then the waiter came with their food, and the sisters fell silent until he was gone again.

Courtney began to cut up her salad. She speared a piece of shrimp and some lettuce leaves, but before putting them into her mouth, she said, "Maybe you should give this new guy at work a chance. Who knows? You might actually like him."

"Who said he's interested in *me?*" P.J. poured a mound of ketchup next to her fries and dipped one in.

Courtney gave her a look. "You're a

very pretty, very sexy woman. Of course he'll be interested in you." She forked another bite of salad into her mouth. Then she grinned. "That's if you can keep your mouth shut."

P.J. glared at her sister. But she couldn't hold the expression and was soon laughing. "Yeah, that *can* be a problem," she admitted. She'd run more than one guy off by expressing her opinions, which were almost always diametrically opposed to theirs.

"So tell me more about this guy," Courtney said when their laughter subsided.

"No point. I'm not interested in him. And even if I *were*, which I'm *not*, he works for me. I don't date guys who work for me. It wouldn't be a good idea."

Courtney nodded. "Yeah, you're probably right. Conflict of interest or something." She studied P.J. for a minute. "Are you sure it's not the baby thing stopping you? Because if it is, lots of guys don't want kids."

P.J. sighed. "I know that." She wanted

to add that any guy who didn't want kids was probably not the kind of guy she'd want to be with, anyway, but she didn't. Courtney would just feel bad if she said something like that.

"Do you? Seems to me you throw up all kinds of excuses to keep men at a distance, and I can't help thinking that's the real reason."

P.J. shrugged. "It's not. But I can't help thinking about it. I mean, what if I start dating someone and really like them and they like me? Then I tell them I can't have kids? Is that fair?"

"Well, you can hardly tell them *before* you go out with them," Courtney pointed out. She made a face. "It *is* a problem, isn't it?"

P.J. nodded, then made a face. "Let's change the subject, okay? I'm awfully tired of this one. Tell me what Jillian and Peter are up to. I haven't talked to either one in weeks."

"The phone works both ways, you know."

P.J. started to laugh. "If my eyes had

been closed, I would have sworn that was Mom talking."

The expression on Courtney's face was priceless. But then she joined P.J.'s laughter, and for the rest of evening, they kept their conversation lighthearted.

Alex had just finished his dinner—a really excellent omelette—and before settling in with the new T. Jefferson Parker book he'd bought, he decided to check his messages on his home phone. He didn't really expect there to be anything important, but he'd better check, anyway.

The first two were invitations he wasn't interested in accepting—he'd ask his secretary to send his regrets—the third was a hangup, and the fourth was from Georgie—short for Georgianna, the oldest of Cornelia's four daughters.

The message started with, "Hey, Alex, where the heck *are* you? I called your office but the call was routed to Marti and she said you're taking a leave of absence? Holy cow, has *hell* frozen over? I've hardly ever known you to leave your precious foundation for a *vacation*, let alone a leave of absence. Call me! I need to talk to you. Smooches."

Alex chuckled. He loved Georgie. Too bad he felt toward her the way he felt toward Julie, because if not, she'd have made a perfect wife.

Punching in the code for her cell, he waited for her to pick up. Instead he got her voice mail. "This is Georgie. Leave a message and I'll call you back soonest."

At the beep, he said, "Hey, girl. It's me, Alex. Call me if you get this message before eleven. After that I'll be racking up Zs. Oh, and I've got a new cell." He gave her the number, then said, "If you don't get home early enough to call back tonight, wait till after four tomorrow, okay?" Not wanting to explain any further, he broke the connection.

Her call back came a little after ten.

"A leave of absence, a new cell, don't call after eleven, don't call during the day… what in the *world* is going on?" she said.

"And hello to you, too," Alex said, grinning. He laid his book on the coffee table, then got up and stretched.

She laughed, the sound low and warm and contagious. "C'mon, quit stalling. Have you joined the CIA or something?"

"Nothing that drastic."

"Well, where *are* you?"

So Alex explained. When he was finished, there was silence for a long moment. Then she said, "I cannot believe this. I especially can't believe my mother went along with it. I mean, Alex, this is the craziest scheme I've ever heard."

"Maybe not that crazy."

"What do you mean, not that crazy? This is the twenty-first century, not the eighteenth." Her voice was indignant. "And giving you a *time* limit? It's blackmail, that's what it is."

"Yes, I guess it is, but—"

"But nothing. I'm going to have a serious talk with Mother. I always knew she was blind as far as your father is concerned, but this is the limit."

Alex couldn't help grinning at Georgie's anger on his behalf. She was nothing if not loyal. "Calm down, okay? I admit, I was ticked off at first, but I'm actually okay with it now." An image of P.J. and the way she'd looked in the park earlier flashed through his mind. "I think it might work out well."

"Wait a minute. Are you saying you've found somebody already?"

He laughed. "I wouldn't go that far. But there are some possibilities."

"So you're saying you're no longer free to meet me for lunch during the week?" Georgie worked for an ad agency in downtown Seattle, and they'd fallen into the habit of meeting for lunch at least once a week.

"No, afraid not."

"How about dinner?"

"Dinner I can do."

"How about tomorrow night?"

"Where?"

She named a restaurant they'd frequented in the past. Luckily it was on the

Portland side of Seattle, so Alex wouldn't have as much traffic to contend with.

"It'll have to be an early night, since I'll have a long drive back," he said.

"How early?"

"Seven?"

"That's doable. I'll see you then. Oh, and Alex?"

"Yes?"

"Despite what you said, I'm *still* going to give Mother a piece of my mind!"

## Chapter Four

By the end of his first week, Alex felt like an old pro at his job. He knew where the most popular products were located without having to look at his diagram, and even when he did have to look, it didn't take him long to find what he needed, get it off the shelf, and fill the order. In fact, he worked almost as fast as Rick did.

"You're doing a great job," Rick said, clapping him on the back late Friday afternoon. They'd both been asked to stay until five because of a huge order that had come in right before their shift was about to end. "You filled as many orders as I did today."

Alex smiled. "Thanks."

Even P.J. gave him a compliment, saying, "You've caught on fast, Alex."

It was absurd how pleased he was by their praise, especially P.J.'s. Maybe she was beginning to trust him. She didn't seem to be watching him as much as she had those first few days.

He'd been watching her, though. He couldn't seem to help it. And the more he watched her, the more intrigued he became, and the more he entertained the possibility of her as a potential wife.

She had just walked by the aisle where he was working when Rick approached from the other end. Alex hoped the younger man hadn't seen him staring at P.J.

But Rick's gaze was guileless. "Hey man, it's quitting time."

Alex looked at his watch. It was after

five. The time had gone so fast that afternoon, he hadn't realized how late it was.

"I wanted to tell you that we usually stop off at Jake's for a couple of beers on Fridays," Rick said. "Want to come?"

"Who's we?"

"Just a bunch of us from the different departments. Mostly singles."

Alex wondered if P.J. would be there. "Okay, sure. Sounds good. Uh, does the boss usually go, too?" He inclined his head in the direction of P.J.'s office.

"Sometimes. Not always. But even if she *does* show up, she's pretty low-key when she's there. She doesn't act like the boss or anything."

"That's good," Alex said for Rick's benefit.

"Some of the guys stay and eat," Rick said as they walked out to the parking lot together. "Jake's has great fried shrimp and onion rings, but me, I gotta get home. Maria's mother is visiting and she said she'd babysit tonight if me and Maria want to catch a movie or something.

Maria's all excited." He grinned. "Thing is, we don't get out much."

Alex had seen Jake's Grill on his drive back and forth to work. Located on River Street, it was only about five minutes from the distribution center. Although it had been raining earlier in the day, the sun had broken through the clouds by the time he reached the five-year-old red Ford pickup truck he'd purchased to conform with his new status in life.

He grinned as he unlocked the driver's-side door. He actually liked the truck. Hell, he might even keep it when this masquerade was over.

After getting in, he rolled down the window. He also liked fresh air. In his capacity as Managing Director of the Harrison Hunt Foundation, when he wasn't sitting on his butt in the office, he spent a lot of time traveling to various facilities. That was the hardest part about his job at the distribution center—having to be indoors all day long.

The drive to Jake's was short. When he

got there, the parking lot was already half-full, even though it was early by most standards. He parked the pickup, locked it and strode toward the entrance.

The inside of Jake's sported dark woods, dart boards on the far wall, and long tables rather than booths. Alex smiled at the player piano cranking out "The Entertainer" and the pretty waitresses in their short black skirts and white blouses. He saw there was also a juke box and some video games on the far wall.

Spying Rick at a long table near the bar, he walked over to join the HuntCom group. He'd met most of them already. A quick glance told him if P.J. was coming, she hadn't made it yet.

"Hey, Alex," Rick said. Sliding his chair over, he made room for Alex to join them. "You know everyone?"

"I don't believe *we've* met," said a striking blonde sitting on the other side of Rick. "I'm Carrie Wancheck. I work in payroll."

"Alex Noble," Alex said, leaning over to

shake her hand. "I've seen you around." He was almost certain she was one of the women who had checked him out during his first couple of days on the job.

She was very pretty, but too young for him, nearer his sister's age than his. He guessed she was probably in her early twenties. He knew a lot of men who had married women fifteen and twenty years younger than them—in fact, the older the men, the more they seemed to like young women. But he wanted someone who wasn't a kid. Someone with ideas, who maybe read the newspaper and had opinions on more than fashions and movies.

*Someone like P.J.*

The thought came unbidden, almost surprising him. Yet he knew it had been brewing for a while.

"So how do you like working at HuntCom?" Carrie asked.

"I like it fine."

She smiled. "And we certainly like having you."

Her tone left no doubt that she was flirting with him. "Thanks," he answered casually. "It seems like a good place to work."

"You want a beer?" Rick said, pushing his chair back and standing.

"Yeah, but I can go get it. Or wait for the waitress to bring me one."

"Okay. Enjoy. I've gotta get going or Maria will kill me."

There were good-natured mutters of "henpecked" and "who wears the pants in your family, Rick?" as he headed for the bar.

The moment he was gone, Carrie slid over onto his vacated seat. She smiled up at Alex. "So I hear you're from Sacramento?"

"Not from Sacramento. I was born in the San Diego area."

That was actually true. Alex's mother had been visiting friends in La Jolla when her water broke—three weeks early—and she gave birth to Alex there. Without Harry's presence, as she had bitterly said more than once.

"I worked in Sacramento before moving here, though." Alex felt he could carry this myth off without tripping himself up because he'd spent a couple of weeks in Sacramento in the course of doing the foundation's work.

"What made you come to this area?"

"My brothers all live around here." *Now why did he say that?*

"Brothers?" Her eyes met his coyly. "Are they all as good-looking as you are?"

Alex was saved from having to answer by Rick's reappearance. "Hey," he said to Carrie. "You stole my seat."

She grinned. "Yes, I did."

He made a face at Alex, handed him his beer—Miller on tap—and sat in her old seat.

"You guys want to hear a joke?" said one of the men on the other side of the table.

"Is it clean? There are ladies present," someone else—Alex thought his name was Mike—said.

"Ladies?" the jokester countered, laughing. "I don't see no ladies."

"Hey, watch it," Carrie said.

"Oh. Didn't see you there, Carrie," he answered with a mock frown.

The banter continued and Alex was able to turn his attention away from Carrie without being rude, but when Rick got up a few minutes later, saying he had to leave, she put her hand on Alex's arm and leaned closer.

"I know a much quieter and nicer place where we could have some privacy." Her smile was suggestive. "And they have much better food."

Alex was taken off-guard and for a moment and couldn't think how to answer her. "Thanks, Carrie, but I have to be going myself."

She pouted. "Oh, *do* you? Darn. I was really hoping to get to know you better."

And Alex had been hoping to have dinner *there*, with the others, especially if P.J. should show up, but now there was no way he could. *Damn.* He'd have to figure out a way to head little Miss Carrie off at the pass. She wasn't even being subtle about her intentions. But she was definitely too young for him, no matter how pretty and sexy she was. More important, he couldn't imagine his aunt approving of someone like her, even if he *were* interested.

After draining his beer, he stood. "Have a good weekend, everyone. I've got to be going, too."

"Sure you won't change your mind?" Carrie asked.

Alex just shook his head and said his goodbyes, making a quick exit.

As he drove home to his apartment, he wondered if J.T. and Gray were faring any better than he was in finding a suitable candidate to be the next Mrs. Hunt. Justin, of course, had already found his—the mother of his year-old daughter, Ava. A daughter Justin'd had no idea even existed, because Lily, Ava's mother and Justin's former lover, had never told him about her after their breakup.

Alex smiled thinking of Ava. He hadn't met his niece yet but he'd seen a photo of her, and she was a winner. With her dark hair and dimples, she was clearly a Hunt. In fact, she looked exactly like Justin. And from the look on Harry's face when he'd seen that photo, she'd already captured *his* heart.

For a moment when Justin had told them about Lily, Ava's mother, Alex had hoped Harry would drop the challenge for the rest of them. After all, he had his much-coveted grandchild now. But no such luck. Harry had only said the rest of them had better get busy.

Alex knew he'd have to make up his mind soon. Pick one of the women he'd met or make an effort to meet someone new. It was already entering the second week of September and he needed a bride *and* a baby on the way by next July.

What would Harry do if one of the brides wasn't pregnant by July? Hell, there were no guarantees. Surely the old man would be fair. If they'd fulfilled their part by marrying suitable women, surely Harry would give them some leeway on the pregnancy question.

But what if he didn't?

What if, after finding brides, they ended by losing their stakes in Harry's empire, anyway?

P.J. was just about to walk out the door when her cell phone rang. Checking the number, she saw it was her brother.

She pressed the talk button. "Hey, Peter, what's up?"

"Nothing much. Just haven't talked to you in a couple of weeks and thought I'd better see if you were still alive."

Why was it Peter always made her feel guilty? "I've been busy. For some reason, lots of people have decided they need Hunt products this month."

"So business is good?"

"Very good."

"And you still like that…job?"

"I still like my job." Peter asked the same questions every time they talked. It was as if he couldn't believe anyone could possibly enjoy the kind of work she did. He was always telling her she was wasting her education, not to mention her brain. His lack of respect for what she did used to make P.J. mad. Now she just patiently gave him the same answers and ignored his jabs.

"Allison said to tell you hello. She's looking forward to seeing you at Dad's birthday dinner next week."

P.J.'s father would turn seventy the following Saturday and they were celebrating with a big family dinner at her parents' home.

"I still haven't figured out what to buy him," she said. "He has everything. What're you and Allison giving him?"

Peter laughed. "You're not going to believe this."

"What?"

"A guitar."

"A guitar!"

"It was Allison's idea."

P.J. was laughing now, too. "Did he *say* he wanted a guitar?"

"Nope. But you know how he is. A total workaholic. Allison said he needed something to do that was relaxing and fun. A hobby of some kind. So we settled on a guitar. I mean, he used to like Dylan. I actually heard him listening to Dylan's music once."

P.J. was still laughing. "Maybe I should arrange for him to have some lessons."

"That's a good idea."

"Think so? Okay, then. I will." Somehow she didn't think her father was going to be pleased, but she had to hand it to Allison and Peter. They had guts.

"So what are you doing tonight?" Peter asked. "Got a hot date?"

P.J. snorted. "Yeah. Sure. Actually, I was just getting ready to join some of the guys from work at a local pub."

"I won't keep you then. See you next week, okay?"

They said their goodbyes, and P.J. finished clearing off her desk, then headed out the door. Fifteen minutes later, she walked into Jake's Grill. Quickly scanning the crowded room, she spied the group from HuntCom.

Even as she told herself she wasn't looking for him, her gaze traveled around the group to see if Alex was there. When she didn't see him, she told herself she wasn't disappointed. If anything, she was relieved.

But she knew she was lying.

"Hey, P.J. 'Bout time you got here." This came from Mike Fields, who worked out at the docks.

Everyone scooted their chairs to make room for her, and P.J. grabbed an empty chair from another table and squeezed in between Carrie Wancheck and Chick Fogarty.

She motioned to a nearby waitress. "I'll have a bottle of Beck's, Jessie."

"Sure thing, P.J."

Carrie nudged P.J.'s arm. "You just missed Alex."

P.J.'s traitorous heart skipped a beat. "Alex who?"

"Oh, c'mon, P.J. Alex Noble. Your new *sexy* employee. Don't tell me you haven't noticed."

"Oh. Him."

"Yeah, him. I tried to persuade him to go to Costello's with me, but he had to leave."

P.J. pretended indifference. "Maybe he had a date."

Carrie frowned. "Think so?"

"A man like him? I don't see him sitting home on a Friday night."

"Shoot. You're probably right. Well, I'm not giving up. Guys like Alex don't come along every day."

"You know, Carrie, he really *is* a lot older than you are. And you don't know anything about him."

"He's gorgeous, he's well-spoken, he smells good, and he has a fantastic smile. I mean, those *dimples!*" Carrie sighed. "The only thing he *doesn't* have is money."

P.J. refrained from rolling her eyes. "How do you know that?"

"Oh, please. As if he'd be working as a picker if he *did*. I mean, come on, P.J."

Not for the first time, P.J. wondered

what her co-workers would think if they knew about her and her family. Then again, she knew what they'd think. It was the reason she'd decided to use initials instead of her first name, which was Paige, when she'd come to work for HuntCom.

P.J. wanted to be treated like everyone else, and if they'd known she was the daughter of Peter Prescott Kincaid and— until she'd repudiated it—heiress to a multimillion-dollar trust fund, there was no way she'd be one of the guys the way she was now.

"Well, money or not, he's still too old for you," P.J. said.

"He's not *that* old. I'm guessing he's in his early thirties."

"Thirty-six." P.J. had checked his application.

"So? That's only fifteen years older than me. Big deal."

"He might have an ex-wife and ten kids."

"Oh, please," Carrie said, rolling her eyes.

P.J. could see that nothing she said was going to head Carrie off. She had set her sights on Alex, and she wasn't going to be persuaded otherwise.

*And why should you care?*

She *didn't* care. As a thirty-year-old, more experienced woman, she just felt she should look out for the younger women at work, that's all.

But even as she told herself this, P.J. knew she was lying to herself. For some reason, Alex Noble intrigued her. More than intrigued her.

*Admit it, you're attracted to him.*

Even though there was something about him that just didn't add up and even though she'd told Courtney she didn't believe in dating an employee and even though she knew there'd be no future in it—how could there be, given her situation?—she knew if Alex Noble were to ask her out, she would want to say yes.

But it would be madness. Absolute madness. Dating Alex Noble would do nothing but cause trouble for her.

So, regretfully, even if he *were* to ask her out, she would have to say no.

## Chapter Five

Now that he was almost home, Alex wasn't sure he really wanted to go there. So what *did* he want to do? He was hungry, but he didn't feel like stopping at any of the restaurants he'd seen and eating by himself. Nor did he feel like cooking tonight, although cooking was one of his passions.

Normally he loved cooking for himself, and he never minded eating alone. But tonight…tonight he wanted company.

*Oh, hell, admit it. You're lonely.*

He wondered what his brothers would say if he ever admitted this to them. They all seemed perfectly happy to be single. Well, maybe not Justin anymore. Now that Lily, the mother of his child, was back in his life, he seemed different. Alex knew without being told that calling Lily when he first knew he had to find a bride quickly was one of the best decisions Justin had ever made. It was obvious that he cared about her. Alex didn't know the background of the two of them—only that they'd been lovers at one time.

But J.T. and Gray? They were stereotypical, self-possessed and self-absorbed bachelors—J.T. with his island and Gray with his business interests.

Alex had always known he was different from his brothers, and this deep-seated loneliness had always isolated him even more. Part of Alex knew the loneliness would only be assuaged by having someone to share his life, someone who loved him unconditionally. He also knew he probably wouldn't feel this way if he'd had that kind of love from either his mother or Harry.

*Don't go there.*

Alex forced himself to stop thinking about what he didn't have in his life. Long ago he'd made up his mind that he wasn't going to feel sorry for himself. Instead, he would build the kind of life he wanted with the kinds of people he wanted to be around, and he would be content with that. But no matter how many times he'd reinforced his goals, he couldn't seem to erase that bone-deep loneliness that always seemed to be waiting for him anytime he lowered his guard.

Tonight was one of those nights.

In an effort to put off the time when he'd have to face his empty apartment, Alex decided to stop at the bookstore he'd noticed in a shopping center a block over from his street. He was just about out of reading material and he knew Greg Isles had a new book out, one Alex was looking forward to reading.

After killing three-quarters of an hour and spending more than a hundred bucks on books, Alex's stomach began to grumble. Time to head home. But as he walked out to the parking lot, he spied a Thai restaurant he hadn't noticed before. He loved Thai food and hadn't had any in weeks.

Abruptly changing his mind about going home, he switched direction and headed for the entrance to the restaurant.

Alex finished some really excellent hot and sour soup and an order of crispy egg rolls and settled back into his booth to wait for his entree. He was glad he'd decided to eat at the restaurant rather than getting takeout. Even though he was alone, he felt better here than he would have in his empty apartment.

He sipped at his Singha beer and idly watched the other diners: an Oriental family of four with exceptionally well-behaved young boys, a college-age couple who were obviously lovers, a middle-aged couple who kept smiling at each other, and a table of four seniors who were laughing and talking like old friends.

Alex felt wistful as he watched.

A moment later, the bell on the front door jangled as a new customer walked in. Alex looked up. Blinked. And looked closer. Yes, that was definitely P.J. approaching the hostess. He watched as she picked up one of the takeout menus and studied it.

In his second impulsive act of the evening, he slid from the booth and walked to the front.

She looked up at his approach. The expression that flitted across her face—which she quickly banished—gave Alex the distinct feeling she was as pleased to see him as he was to see her.

"Hey, P.J.," he said.

"Hi, Alex."

"You placing a takeout order?"

"That's the plan."

The hostess, a pretty girl who looked about seventeen, looked curiously from one to the other.

"How about joining me instead?"

P.J. hesitated, and for a moment, Alex thought she was going to refuse. Then she smiled. "Actually, I wouldn't mind company. I'm really not much in the mood to eat alone."

"Good. I'm not, either."

He led her to his booth and waited until she slid in across from him before taking his seat. The pretty hostess had followed them and she handed P.J. a menu. "I'll send your waiter," she said before leaving them.

P.J. glanced at the menu, then set it aside. "So how are you liking your job now that you've been with us a while?"

Alex was glad he could answer truthfully. "I'm enjoying it a lot."

"That's good. I confess, I'm surprised."

"Surprised? Why?"

"You just don't seem the type to be working at the center."

"What type is that?"

She leaned back, a smile teasing the edges of her mouth. "I had you pegged for a college man. You seem much better suited to a white-collar job."

"I could say the same about you."

"Oh, really?"

Alex returned her smile. "Yes, really."

"Well, you'd be wrong. My job suits me perfectly."

"You certainly do it well."

Once again, that pleased expression flitted across her face. "Thank you."

"You're welcome."

Just then, their waiter approached.

"I'll have what he's having," P.J. said, pointing to Alex's bottle of beer.

"And I'll have another," Alex said.

"I also want the pad thai," P.J. said.

Alex grinned. "I already ordered some. Want to get something different and we can share?"

"Sure. How about the green curry chicken?"

"Great."

Once the waiter had gone, P.J. settled back again and said, "So where were we?"

"Saying neither one of us looks the type

to be working in a big warehouse." Alex figured he might as well be up-front about her comment. No sense pretending it hadn't been said.

She studied him thoughtfully. "*Did* you ever go to college?"

"Yes."

"And?"

"And what?"

"And...did you get your degree?"

Keeping to his promise to himself that he would tell the truth whenever he could, Alex said, "Yes, as a matter of fact, I did." He didn't think he needed to add that he'd also gotten a master's degree.

"So what happened?"

"I didn't like the business world." Alex still didn't like the business world. Thank God he didn't have to be a part of it.

"I didn't like the business world, either," she said.

"What did *you* study in college?"

"What makes you think I went to college?"

"Oh, c'mon, P.J. It's as plain as the nose

on your face. You're obviously well educated."

She shrugged. "On my father's recommendation, I was in public relations. I hated every minute of it."

Alex chuckled. "How long did you last?"

"Oh, I got my degree. My parents would have disowned me if I hadn't. But when I decided to take an entry-level blue-collar job at HuntCom, my father went ballistic." She smiled crookedly. "He still doesn't understand me."

Alex thought about Harry. Maybe *all* fathers were destined not to understand their children. Harry certainly was batting zero. "So how did you end up at HuntCom?"

"Through a friend of a friend."

Alex would have liked to question her further, but their waiter had just walked up with their beers. A moment later, he returned with Alex's pad thai.

"Dig in," he said when the waiter left.

They ate companionably for a few

minutes, then P.J. said, "I apologize if I gave you a hard time at first."

"You didn't give me a hard time."

"Yes, I did."

He grinned around a fork full of food. "Okay, you did. But that's okay. You were just doing your job."

She looked at him for a long moment. "I was worried you might be a spy," she confessed.

"A spy!" Alex laughed. "What kind of a spy?"

"You know. A corporate spy. Somebody sent to see if I was doing a good job or something."

Something in those blue eyes of hers told Alex she might still harbor that suspicion. "Listen, P.J., I swear to you, I am *not* a spy."

She nodded.

Alex started to say he was just a regular guy who wanted to do a good job, but that wasn't really true, was it? When and if she found out who he *really* was, she would remember how he'd looked her in the eye and lied to her. And even though Alex wasn't sure how he felt about P.J. Kincaid or whether she'd ever assume more importance in his life than she did at this moment, he didn't want her to think ill of him. *Damn.* This pretending to be someone he wasn't was more complicated than Alex had envisioned it being.

"Here comes our curry chicken," she said, saving him from having to say anything more.

After the waiter finished serving them and had walked off once more, P.J. said, "You have any family around here, Alex?" She spooned some rice onto her plate, then helped herself to the curry.

He nodded. "My brothers all live in the area, and my parents are in Seattle. What about you?"

"My family all live around here, too." She took a bite. "Umm, that's good."

Alex liked the way she enjoyed her food. He got tired of women who never seemed to eat anything but salad. "Their food is good."

"Yeah, I get takeout here about once a week." She grinned. "If you're interested, I know all the great takeout places in Jansen. I know a fantastic pizza place as well as the best Italian restaurant in town."

"Actually, I like to cook."

"You're kidding."

He shook his head. "Nope. Cooking is probably the thing that gives me the greatest pleasure." Next to his work at the Hunt Foundation, but of course, he couldn't say that.

"I can't even boil water." She laughed. "Once I burned the coffee."

Alex laughed, too. "Cooking's easy. If you can read, you can cook. You just follow the directions."

She rolled her eyes. "That's easy for you to say. You like it. Believe me, I've tried. Not only am I a terrible cook, but I hated it. I mean, why bother when you can get food like this?" She waved her fork at the serving dishes. "Are you going to eat the rest of that pad thai?"

"No, I'm full."

"Oh, good." Reaching for the platter, she scraped the remainder of the noodle dish onto her plate.

Yes, a *very* healthy appetite, Alex thought. He wondered if that appetite extended to other areas of her life. Somehow he imagined it might. P.J. seemed like the kind of woman who would thoroughly enjoy sex.

As if she knew what he'd been thinking, a faint flush crept into her cheeks as their eyes met and held.

She was the first one to look away, and Alex knew he'd flustered her.

"That was great," she said, putting down her fork and lifting her napkin to her mouth.

"Yes," he said. "Thank you for joining me." He motioned to their waiter.

"Are you finished?" the waiter said.

"I think so, unless the lady wants dessert?"

P.J. shook her head. "No, just the check."

The waiter said he'd be right back.

"I don't want an argument over the check," she said. "I'm paying for my share."

"No, you're not," Alex said. "I invited you to join me, it's my treat."

"Look, Alex—"

"I insist," Alex said.

P.J. argued a few more seconds, then finally relented.

The waiter returned, laying a leather folder by Alex. Alex reached back and pulled his wallet out of his back pocket. Opening it, he automatically reached for his platinum American Express card, but at the last second, he remembered that he wasn't Alex Hunt tonight, he was Alex Noble, and he took out his new Visa card instead. Close call, he thought, as he slipped the card into the leather folder.

When he looked up, P.J. was watching him. Damn. Had she *seen* that card? If she'd been looking at his wallet when he'd opened it, she probably had. Worse, she would have seen that he had several platinum cards. What would she make of that information?

*I'm going to have to remember to be more careful. She's way too observant.*

The waiter came by again and picked up the folder. P.J. excused herself to go to the ladies' room and was gone when the waiter returned. Alex took care of filling in the tip and signing the charge slip, then went to the front of the restaurant to wait for her.

When they walked outside, the sun had set and there was now a decided chill in the air.

"Summer fades fast in this neck of the woods," Alex said.

"Yes," P.J. agreed. She stopped next to a little blue Miata. "Thank you for dinner. I enjoyed it."

Alex smiled. "My pleasure."

She opened the driver's-side door. "See you Monday."

He waited till she'd gotten into the car before walking to his truck. Would Cornelia like P.J.? Alex wondered. He thought she would. In fact, there were things about P.J. that reminded him of

Cornelia. Not that they looked alike. Although Cornelia was a tall woman and so was P.J., that was the extent of their physical similarities. Cornelia was more delicately built and in her youth had had pale blond hair whereas P.J.'s coloring was more vivid. But both were strong-willed, intelligent and independent.

Yes. Cornelia would approve of P.J.

Alex smiled as he climbed into his truck. He had a feeling Georgie would, too, even though she still remained adamant that this whole bride hunt was ridiculous and had followed through on her promise to tell her mother exactly what she thought.

Not that Georgie's objections had made any difference to either Cornelia or Alex.

He wasn't a hundred-percent certain, but he was beginning to believe he might have found the woman he wanted.

P.J. pulled into the circular drive in front of the stately home where she'd grown up and cut the ignition. Reaching for the small gift bag that contained a couple of oldies CDs and the gift card for a dozen guitar lessons with the best instructor she could find in the Seattle area, she got out of the Miata and walked up to the massive oak front door and rang the bell.

"Miss Paige, you know you can just come on in," Carmelita, the family's long-time housekeeper said as she opened the door. "You're family." Leaning over, she kissed P.J.'s cheek.

P.J. inhaled the scent of talcum and gave Carmelita a hug.

"Everyone's back in the solarium," Carmelita said. "You go on and join them. I'll have Marianne bring you some lemonade."

P.J. headed for the dome-topped, semicircular room that overlooked Puget Sound. As she approached the solarium, she heard the cheerful noises of her rapidly expanding family.

"Paige!" her mother exclaimed as P.J. walked into the room. Getting up, Helena Kincaid held out her arms. Hugging her mother was vastly different from hugging cushiony Carmelita. Helena, like most women in her social class, was reed-thin and smelled of the most expensive beauty products on the market. Although dressed casually, there was no mistaking the designer slacks in a soft fawn wool or the meticulously crafted cream silk blouse as anything but the best money could buy.

"Darling, it's so good to see you," her mother said, releasing her and holding her at arm's length. "I do wish you'd buy yourself some decent clothes, though." She eyed P.J.'s denim skirt and white T-shirt with distaste.

P.J. had learned to ignore her mother's critiques. "Well, *you* look lovely, Mom," was all she said. Then she turned to greet the rest of her family.

Jillian, younger by three years, grinned at her. The grin said she was glad P.J. was the object of their mother's scrutiny instead of her. As they hugged, she murmured, "She's in rare form today."

"Thanks for the warning."

After that, P.J. got hugs in quick succession from Matt, Jillian's husband; Courtney and Brad; her father; Peter and his wife, Allison; and then all the nieces and nephews she could corral.

"So what's new, Paige?" Allison asked after the men had wandered off to the den to watch the Mariners game.

"Same old, same old," P.J. said. "Thanks, Marianne," she said to the maid, who had brought her a tall glass of the homemade lemonade she was famous for.

"Any new men in your life?" Allison continued. Her dark eyes were filled with lively curiosity.

P.J. gave her sister-in-law a dark look. Why was it that one of the first questions out of everyone's mouth had to do with men?

Allison laughed. "I take it that's a no."

P.J. shrugged. "Take it any way you like."

Allison raised her eyebrows. "Hear that, Courtney? Jillian? Sounds like maybe there *is* a new man on the horizon."

P.J. tried not to think about Alex but she couldn't help it. And thinking about him made her blush. Oh, God, she'd give anything not to have the pale skin of a redhead. Skin that showed every single emotion.

"Tell us everything," Jillian said excitedly.

*Hell and damnation. I don't need this.*

P.J. made a face. "There is no new man. I don't know what you're talking about."

"Well, *something* made you blush," Jillian said.

"*Are* you dating someone, Paige?" her mother said.

"No, mother, I'm not."

"You know, Paige, you aren't getting any younger."

P.J.'s eyes met Courtney's. Courtney's eyes sparkled, and it was obvious she was trying hard not to laugh.

"Mom, please…"

"Well, it's true," Helena said. "And there's absolutely no reason for you to still be single. Why, even Liliana Fox is engaged, and no one thought she'd *ever* find a man. You're just too picky, that's all. When I think about Douglas…" Her voice trailed off in despair.

Douglas Sloane Bryant was the son of P.J.'s parents' oldest friends, Liz and Oliver Bryant, and at one time, he and P.J. had dated. This was before P.J.'s medical problems, before she knew she could probably never have any children of her own. Of course, her mother *still* didn't know it, and if P.J. had her way, she never would. That's all she needed—unsolicited medical advice from her mother. In fact, the only person in her family who did know was Courtney, and that's how P.J. wanted to keep it.

At the time P.J. had dated Douglas, if she'd given him any encouragement at all, he would probably have produced the obligatory diamond ring, but even though she'd liked him as a friend, there was absolutely no passion between them and no sense pretending otherwise.

Plus he worked in his father's business.

As the Chief Financial Officer. And he was totally into status. He and his wife—he'd married last year—had built a six-thousand-square-foot home on Bainbridge Island. Now who needed six thousand square feet?

"And how you expect to meet anyone suitable working in the kind of place you do," her mother droned on, "is beyond me. If you'd only stop being so stubborn and—"

"I told you, Mom," P.J. interrupted. "I have no interest in meeting someone *suitable*...or in getting married. And I'm tired of people harassing me."

Her mother sniffed. "As your mother, I feel I have a perfect right to—"

"No, Mom," P.J. interrupted again, "you *don't* have a right to continually berate me about getting married. I have a right to make my own choices."

"Yes, well, if your choices were sensible..."

P.J. sighed. What was the use? Her mother would never change. "Tell you what, Mom. If I meet someone *suitable*, you'll be the first to know. Okay? And in the meantime, let's just drop the subject. Otherwise, I'm going to just leave Dad's gift here and take off." So saying, she got to her feet.

"Oh, Paige, sit down," her mother said. She sighed dramatically. "Fine. I won't say another word." She made a motion as if she was turning a key to lock her mouth. "Happy now?"

P.J. grinned. "That's two words, Mom."

Their laughter broke the tension, and for the remainder of the afternoon, no more was said about P.J. or her personal life.

## Chapter Six

Monday turned out to be Alex's busiest day at the HuntCom Distribution Center since he'd begun the job. There was barely time to breathe, let alone take a break. And lunch consisted of a sandwich gobbled in ten minutes. He was in the middle of filling a large order for an office supply store in Portland when his cell phone vibrated.

"Dammit," he muttered. Checking the caller ID, he saw it was J.T. He almost let the call go to voice mail, then decided it must be important because J.T. rarely called him.

Alex pressed the talk button. "Hang on." Moving away from the noise of a nearby forklift, he said, "There must be a problem if you're calling me at work."

"'Work' is eighty miles north of here," J.T. said. "What you're doing is...what *are* you doing, anyway?"

Alex laughed. "Filling orders."

"Right. Look, there's no problem. I just need to talk to you. I'm over at the expansion site."

"You're in Jansen?"

"Yes. I just finished a site inspection with the construction foreman. Which warehouse are you in?"

Alex lowered his voice. "Don't come over here. If somebody recognizes you, they might recognize me. I get off at four. Meet me at my place at four-thirty."

"Where's that?"

Alex gave J.T. directions. "Don't be surprised by the place. It's not what you're used to," he said in warning. That was an understatement, he thought after they'd hung up. He'd seen Gray's place in town and he figured J.T. and Justin probably lived in places just as luxurious when they happened to be in the city—which wasn't often. That was one of the reasons Alex hadn't seen either place—the other being that unfortunately, he and his half-brothers weren't close, something Alex was beginning to hope might change one of these days.

On the dot of four-thirty, a knock sounded at Alex's front door. He opened it and smiled at J.T. The brothers weren't close, yet there was a bond that couldn't be denied.

"Hey," J.T. said, stepping in.

"Hey, J.T."

J.T. glanced around. "When Gray said you'd taken a job at the warehouse as a cover for this bride thing, he didn't mention that you'd moved in with the masses."

Alex laughed. "When in Rome…"

"In Rome, they at least live with some color." J.T's thoughtful frown moved from the breakfast bar that separated the small kitchen from the living area. He took in the beige sofa, nondescript coffee table and black leather recliner, which formed what there was of Alex's seating area. "You could seriously use some art here," he observed. "Did the furniture come with the place?"

Alex shook his head. "I bought it at a discount store. If anyone from the plant comes over, I don't want them to suspect anything."

"Any luck there? Meeting an appropriate woman, I mean?"

Alex gave a guarded shrug. "I've only been there three weeks," he said evasively. He wasn't ready to talk about P.J.

"Then you've spotted a prospect?"

"It's too soon to tell. I don't have much of a liquor supply," he added, not bothering to be subtle about the change of subject. Alex wasn't ready to talk about P.J. to anyone. "About all I can offer you is a beer." He nodded toward the kitchen. "Do you want one?"

J.T. grinned. "Let me guess. You bought it on sale, $3.99 for a twelve-pack."

Alex smiled sheepishly. "There are a few things I still splurge on. I have Beck's or Black Sheep."

"Surprise me."

"So," Alex said as he swung open the refrigerator door. "Why'd you want to see me?"

"I need some advice."

Alex turned from the refrigerator, a bottle in each hand and one eyebrow arched. "From me?" He couldn't remember the last time one of his brothers wanted his advice.

From where he remained on the other side of the bar, J.T. frowned. "You're the only person I know who knows anything about fund-raisers."

"What makes you think I know about fund-raisers?"

"Hell, Alex. You go to them all the time. And you have to raise money for the foundation somehow."

"That shows how little we know about what each of us does," Alex informed him. "You're right about one thing. I've attended a lot of fund-raisers for different charities or organizations, but the Harrison Hunt Foundation doesn't raise money that way." He popped off the caps with a bottle opener and held a bottle out for J.T. "We use the interest from Harry's money to fund our causes." And occasionally they accepted donations from other parties, but that wasn't relevant, so there was no point in bringing it up. "What is it you want to know about them?"

"The short version is that I want to help someone raise some money."

"And the long version?"

J.T. tipped up his bottle and drank. Alex wondered if he wanted to buy time before answering, because there was something about his expression that seemed wary.

"This bride-hunt thing," J.T. finally said. "Because of Harry's rules, I can't just write a check. Or," he added with a half-smile, "go to my brother and ask the foundation to do it. If I did that, I'm afraid she'd figure out the money had something to do with me." The smile died. "If she did, I could tell her I just happened to know someone with connections, but I don't want to raise any red flags."

Curious now, Alex rounded the counter and pulled out a bar stool. Motioning for J.T. to take the other, he said, "You've found a potential wife?"

J.T. frowned. "How'd you get that from what I just told you?"

"You're talking about helping a woman. You said you can't because of Harry's rules. I'm not the math genius in the family, but it's pretty much one plus one, J.T."

"I've found a woman with the potential to be a wife," J.T. said. He hesitated. "But the woman I want to help is her assistant. Her grandmother lives in this home that's going to have to close if the director can't come up with about fifty grand."

Both of Alex's eyebrows lifted this time. "That's not the kind of money you can raïse selling calendars. You need an event, and a corporation or two to under-write it. Like I said, we don't organize fund-raisers, but I know people who do."

He thought for a moment. "One of women on the foundation board chairs an annual luncheon and fashion show that makes a mint for the Seattle Opera Guild. Maybe your girlfriend's assistant could do something like that in Portland."

"Think she'd be willing to talk to Amy?"

"Amy's the assistant?"

J.T. nodded.

"I can't imagine that she wouldn't."

J.T. seemed relieved. "Let me run this by Amy, then. If she thinks it's something she can handle, I'll get back to you."

"Sure. Not a problem." Alex drank some of his beer. "You hungry?"

"Getting there."

"I'm starving. How about I throw some-thing together for us to eat?"

"What did you have in mind?"

"Paella," he said, heading back into the

kitchen. "I picked up shrimp and sausage at the market last night. That sound okay?"

"You can make paella?"

Alex just shook his head and laughed. J.T., Justin, and Gray were all intelligent, successful men. But their idea of cooking was limited to grilling steaks or chicken.

"Then it sounds great," J.T. said.

As Alex began his preparations with J.T. watching, he tried to remember the last time he'd shared a meal with one of his brothers, and he couldn't.

Harry's bride-hunt idea might be unconventional, perhaps even crazy, but it had accomplished something unexpected. It had brought Alex and his brothers closer together.

And for that, Alex was grateful.

J.T.'s visit had got Alex thinking, and he'd decided he really needed to find out more about P.J. before he made any kind of move—for two reasons. One, even though she seemed to be exactly the kind of woman he wanted, and it was hard to believe she was hiding anything, only a fool would take someone on face value, and he wasn't a fool. Two, if she was already spoken for, he'd have to look elsewhere for his bride.

The first thing he did was Google her. Several items with either the initials *P.J.* or the name *Kincaid* came up, but those didn't apply. Then he saw an article that had appeared in the *Seattle Times* about someone named Paige Jeffers Kincaid.

He clicked on the article, dated April of the previous year. It was a write-up about Peter Prescott Kincaid, CEO of Kincaid Industries, whose ancestors had made fortunes in lumber and shipbuilding. Paige Jeffers Kincaid was one of Peter Kincaid's daughters. At the time the article was written, she was twenty-nine years old.

Alex frowned. Could P.J. be Paige Jeffers Kincaid? The age was about right. Too bad there wasn't a picture with the article.

He went back to the Google home page

and entered *Paige Jeffers Kincaid*. Several items appeared and he scrolled down until he found one with a picture.

The picture accompanied an article about Paige Kincaid's graduation from a private girls' high school where she'd been valedictorian of her class.

The picture showed a fresh-faced, serious-looking P.J. Alex stared at the photo for a long time. The article called her an heiress. "Heiress to a great fortune," it said. "The third of Peter Prescott Kincaid's four children," it said, "who will be attending Stanford in the fall."

At first, he was indignant. What the hell was she *doing,* pretending to be an ordinary woman working at an ordinary job? Before long, though, amusement supplanted the indignation. She was doing exactly what he was doing. How could he be angry with her? He'd be willing to bet every single thing she'd told him had been the truth.

Well, well, well. This changed everything. And yet, did it? After all, if Alex *did* marry P.J., no one could ever accuse her of wanting his money.

So now he knew half of what he needed to know. And he'd just bet Rick could supply the other half. He decided the first chance he got, he would quiz Rick about her.

It was Wednesday before he got the chance. The two of them were eating lunch together in the cafeteria and Rick mentioned something P.J. had said earlier. "Hey," Alex said after he'd finished telling the anecdote, "I've been meaning to ask you. What's P.J.'s story?"

Rick, who had just taken a huge bite of his burger, chewed and swallowed before giving Alex a knowing grin. "I knew you liked her."

"I'm just curious about her. You have to admit, she's not exactly the kind of woman you'd expect to find in a warehouse."

"Yeah," Rick agreed. "I figured out a long time ago she comes from a different background than most of the women at the center. More educated." He looked at Alex speculatively. "Kinda like you."

*"Me?"*

"It's obvious you're a helluva lot more educated than the rest of us, Alex. Lotta the guys been wondering what you're doing at the center."

Alex winced. And here he thought he'd been fitting in so well.

"It's no big deal," Rick continued. "Most of 'em figure you got your reasons for working there. Hell, we all got our reasons. Anyway, I think P.J.'s family probably has some money or something. She pretends she's like the rest of us, but you can tell she comes from a privileged background. I mean, even the way she talks is different, you know? Something must have happened, though," Rick added, "because here she is."

"Happened with her family, you mean?"

"Yeah. Maybe they don't get along."

Alex nodded. Yet on the night he'd met her jogging she'd mentioned having a date with her sister for dinner and the other night at the Thai place she'd said her family all lived in the area. She hadn't sounded as if they were estranged or anything. On the other hand, she might have felt she didn't know him well enough to mention any problems they might have. He certainly hadn't said anything about *his* family. "Does she ever talk about them?"

Rick shook his head. "One time she just said they didn't see eye to eye."

That could have been a reference to the differences she'd mentioned regarding her job choice. Or it could be something deeper. *Maybe she's got a mother like mine.* "How long has she worked for the company?"

"She started about six months before I did. In fact, we worked on the same team for a while."

Alex wondered if Rick had resented the fact P.J. had been promoted to a supervisory position and he hadn't.

"But it was obvious from the beginning she wouldn't stay a picker for long," Rick said. "She's too smart."

"Did you mind that? That she got promoted and you didn't?"

"Me? Hell, no. I don't want to be in management. Nothing but headaches managing people."

Alex smiled. Rick was right. In fact, managing the staff at the foundation was Alex's least favorite part of the job. Thank God for Marti. She was a jewel when it came to getting people to do their jobs without resentment or problems.

"P.J.'s a good boss. Lots better than I would have been," Rick said.

"Wonder why she's not married," Alex commented, keeping his voice casual as he got to what he really wanted to know.

"Now *that* I can answer." Rick grinned. "She doesn't believe in marriage. Said there's no way she's ever gonna let some man order her around."

Alex chuckled in spite of himself. That sounded like P.J. "Think she means it?"

"I've never known P.J. to say anything she doesn't mean."

The words were hardly out of Rick's

mouth when a voice behind Alex said, "Who's taking my name in vain?"

Alex turned around. P.J. stood there, hands on her denim-clad hips, a mock frown on her face.

"We were just sayin' what a great boss you are, boss," Rick said.

P.J. rolled her eyes. "Yeah, right."

"We *were*," Rick insisted.

"Is that true, Alex?" she said.

"Scout's honor," Alex said, raising his right hand.

She fought against the smile, but lost. Soon all three were laughing. "Well, next time you have to fill out one of those surveys about our department, make sure you remember to say that," she said. "Maybe they'll give me a big raise." Then she waved goodbye and left them to their lunch.

"She's a good sport," Rick said.

Alex nodded. He admired the way she treated her employees. She was professional, but she was also friendly. He could tell they respected her. He wondered what they'd think if they knew her background.

"She's also a really nice person," Rick added.

"Seems to be," Alex said.

"No, I mean *really* nice. She's helped out a couple of the people here. Financially, I mean. One of the girls in the shipping department, her little boy was sick and the girl either needed to stay home and take care of him or hire someone to do it and either way, she couldn't afford it. P.J. heard about it and she made sure Evvie was taken care of."

"Taken care of…how?"

"She started a sick-day pool. You know, she convinced the powers that be to let any employee who wanted to to contribute some of their sick days to Evvie so she could stay home and not lose pay. And P.J. contributed the most. Plus I heard she also gave Evvie some money."

The more Rick talked about P.J., the more Alex admired her. It seemed to him that she had exactly the same kinds of values he had. In fact, he couldn't imagine finding another woman more suited to him.

She was the woman he wanted.

Now all he had to do was convince her she really *did* want to be married.

"Hey, Alex, you have any interest in poker?" Rick asked later that afternoon.

"I love poker. Play every chance I get." He'd actually started a poker night with a couple of the guys who worked for the foundation.

"Well, a bunch of us play twice a month, and we're supposed to play tomorrow night, but Chick, who's one of our regulars, can't make it. Wanna fill in?"

"Sure, that'd be great."

"It's at Wayne's house. He'll give you directions."

When Alex walked into Wayne Crowder's house the following evening, the first person he saw was P.J. He could see she was as surprised as he was, even though she tried to disguise it, just as he did. Alex wasn't sure if he was glad or not. Having her there would be a distraction, and Alex took his poker seriously.

Wayne brought Alex a beer and he

joined the others at the table. They were playing in the dining room of the small bungalow, and Wayne had set out bowls of nuts, pretzels and chips.

Alex noticed a high chair in the corner but no sign of a child or a wife. What he'd seen of the house was homey and had a woman's touch, so he figured there must be a female in the equation.

"Let's get started," Rick said. He began to shuffle the cards as the others dug out their money.

"What do you guys play?" Alex asked.

"Texas hold 'em," Wayne said.

"My favorite," Alex said.

"You play much poker, Alex?" The question came from Jim.

"Whenever I get the chance."

Rick explained the rules. "No one's allowed to lose more than twenty dollars. Once your twenty bucks is gone, you gotta just watch."

The first hand was a dud for Alex. Dealt the three of hearts and nine of spades, he immediately folded.

P.J., on the other hand, had a pair of jacks in the hole and when the river card was a third jack, the pot was hers.

"That was nice," she said as she scooped up her winnings.

"For you, maybe," grumbled Jim.

Alex smothered a smile. Most men hated losing to a woman. A lot of women might have made a disparaging remark, saying something like, "Oh, I was just lucky," but not her. She grinned happily, quite obviously pleased with herself.

Of course, considering her background, it didn't surprise him that she had so much self-confidence or that she wasn't falsely modest. It was funny how now that he knew who she really was, he could see evidence of it in everything she said and did.

Rick dealt the next hand. Alex's hole cards were the two red kings. Wayne folded immediately, throwing his cards down in disgust. P.J. bet the minimum and Jim called. Then it was Alex's turn. He had decided not to raise, because he didn't want to give his hand away. He'd wait and see what happened with the flop. "Call," he said.

The flop consisted of the Queen of Spades, the deuce of clubs and the eight of diamonds. P.J. again bid the minimum and Jim raised. Alex called again, and P.J. threw her money in, staying with the hand.

When the turn card was another eight, Jim couldn't disguise his excitement. Alex figured he probably had two eights in the hole. He almost folded, but then threw in his money. He'd stayed this long, he might as well see what the river brought. What it brought was the Queen of Hearts. Disgusted, Alex finally folded. He was certain Jim had a full house.

But to his amazement—and Jim's shock—after two more rounds of bidding and raising, P.J. revealed her hole cards to be the two missing queens.

That hand set the tone for the night. Alex was a good player—a very good player, in fact—yet he was outplayed by P.J., who was not only skillful but lucky, and who ended up the night's big winner.

"See why we're considering making this a men-only night?" Rick said, half-jokingly. "She cleans us out every time."

P.J. grinned. "Better not try it. I have ways of retaliating, you know."

As they got ready to leave, there was the sound of a car in the driveway, and a few minutes later the back door opened. A pretty dark-haired woman holding a sleeping child walked into the dining room.

"Hey, Lauren," chorused the men.

Lauren smiled and said hello. Her gaze moved to Alex.

"Honey," Wayne said, "this is Alex Noble. He works with us. Alex, my wife, Lauren, and that's our rug rat, Billy, sleeping on her shoulder." Wayne's smile was proud. "He was a year old last week."

"Hi, Lauren," Alex said. "Nice to meet you."

By now, P.J. had gotten up and walked over to where Lauren and the baby stood. "Wow, he's grown," she said softly, touching his silky dark hair. Her smile was tender as she peeked at him. "He gets cuter every day."

Lauren smiled and Wayne beamed. "And smarter," Wayne said.

"And more demanding," Lauren said. "He actually thinks he runs this household."

P.J. chuckled. "And I'd be willing to bet he does."

Wayne made a face.

"Well," Rick said. "We'd better be going. Let you people get to bed."

As Alex drove home, he kept thinking about P.J. How she'd looked that night—her face flushed with excitement, her hair tumbling out of its clips, her eyes sparkling. He thought about how they came from similar backgrounds and spoke the same language. He thought about how smart she was and how good with people and what a wicked game of poker she played. But mostly, he thought about how she'd looked and acted toward little Billy. It was obvious she loved kids.

That was a huge factor to Alex, because

even if Harry hadn't made having a child part of the challenge he'd issued, Alex definitely wanted children. In fact, he wanted lots of them.

And from what he'd seen tonight, it looked as if P.J. felt exactly the same way.

## Chapter Seven

Alex walked up the flagstone driveway toward the laughter and noise of his sister's birthday party. He'd much rather have gone to Jake's tonight with the rest of the guys from work, but he'd promised Julie he'd be here.

When he reached the wrought-iron gate, he stood for a moment before opening it and entering. Even then, he didn't head toward the merrymaking, but took a few minutes to observe the crush of guests gathered on the back veranda and around the pool. There were about forty people there, he estimated, most of them his sister's friends. Looking around, he spied Julie, who looked spectacular in a form-fitting black strapless dress, laughing and talking to a group of young people about her age. Suddenly, as if she felt his gaze, she turned.

"Alex!" she cried. "You made it!"

Beaming, she rushed to his side. Putting his arm around her, he kissed her cheek. "Hello, birthday girl."

Her blue eyes shone with excitement. Julie loved nothing better than a party. And a party in her honor was the best of all possible worlds.

Alex handed her the small, silver-wrapped box he carried. "Happy Birthday."

"Thank you! Oh, I love presents." Taking his hand, she led him toward her friends. "C'mon. I want to introduce you."

Alex knew it was useless to protest, so he let himself be led. Six pairs of eyes turned his way.

"This is my gorgeous brother, Alex," Julie said. "Alex, these are…" One by one, she named them. "Crystal, Russ, Scott, Madison, Penn and Phoebe."

The girl named Phoebe, a truly spectacular blonde, gave him a seductive look from under long eyelashes.

"Gorgeous is right," she murmured.

Alex would never get used to the boldness of Julie's crowd. The girls didn't seem to care what they said or how they said it. If they wanted something, they went after it, no holds barred.

Not waiting for Alex to answer, Phoebe slipped her arm through his and said, "He's mine."

The others laughed.

Gently but firmly, Alex removed her arm. "It's nice to have met all of you, but I have to go say hello to my mother." Directing his smile at all of them, he said, "Excuse me."

Shaking his head mentally, he headed toward the house. It was a moment before he realized Julie had hurried after him.

"Alex, wait up!" she said.

He turned around, stopped so she could catch up to him.

"You broke Phoebe's heart," she said as she reached his side.

"I seriously doubt that."

"I've been telling her about you for weeks." Although her tone was scolding, her blue eyes—the same shade as the tourmalines in his gift—were amused.

Alex looked down at her. "Not interested, Jules."

"Why not? Phoebe's beautiful and sexy and rich in her own right. Plus she's my best friend."

"For one thing, she's too young. For another, she's not my type."

"Too young? She's twenty-five! And how could she not be your type? Most men would die to have Phoebe."

Alex wasn't in the mood to spar or to justify his reasons for not wanting to get involved with the model-like Phoebe. "Aren't you going to open your present?" he said instead, for Julie still held his gift.

"Later. I'll put this on the table with the rest of them."

Alex knew his sister was punishing him for not going along with her matchmaking scheme. Or maybe she just wanted to ensure he'd stay at the party for a while.

"Mom's probably over there," Julie said, pointing to the area on the other side of the pool where there were several umbrella-topped tables.

Alex and Julie headed that way. Sure enough, his mother sat at the nearest table along with Julie's father and another older couple. At their approach, Terrence touched his wife's arm, and Lucinda turned around.

Her face lit up, and she rose. As always, she looked beautiful. Tonight she wore an emerald silk pants outfit with wide legs. Her dark hair was swept up, and sizable diamond studs twinkled in her ears. A small woman with a trim figure, she didn't look her fifty-eight years and could have easily passed for someone in her early forties.

As always, Alex felt himself tense as she rushed forward and put her arms around him. Because he was essentially kind and because he did love her, even as he knew he would never be able to trust her, he returned her embrace, saying, "Hello, Mother."

"Oh, Alex, it's so good to see you." She drew back and looked up into his eyes. "You look wonderful."

"You look very nice yourself." He heard how stiff he sounded and wished he could be more generous toward her. But the habits of a lifetime were hard to break, especially when the underlying reason for his feelings hadn't changed.

"Thank you for coming," she said softly, her dark eyes liquid in the deepening light. Her dimples flashed briefly when she smiled.

Alex had inherited his height from Harry, but everything else came from his mother: dark hair, dark eyes, dimples. Julie, on the other hand, looked more like her father than like Lucinda, with her blue eyes, five-foot-eight height, and larger bone structure. The only trait of Lucinda's she bore was the dark, almost black, hair.

"Come meet our friends, darling," Lucinda was saying. She took Alex's hand and led him forward.

"These are Spencer and Deanna Steele. My son, Alex Hunt." There was no denying the pride in her voice as she introduced them.

Alex shook hands with Spencer Steele, a powerful-looking man with gray hair and an enviable physique. He smiled at Deanna Steele, a lovely, cool-looking blonde who had remained seated. He then turned to his stepfather. "Hello, Terrence."

"Glad you could make it, Alex," Terrence said.

"Alex just met Phoebe," Julie said, addressing the remark to the Steeles. Turning to Alex, she said, "Spencer and Deanna are Phoebe's parents." Her eyes twinkled mischievously.

Alex decided he would not let his sister

get to him. "You have a very beautiful daughter," he said graciously.

"Yes," Deanna said, "we think so." Her gaze was speculative.

They made polite conversation for a few more minutes, and all the while Alex was wondering how long he'd have to stand there before he could make his escape.

"What do you do, Alex?" Spencer Steele asked.

"I'm the CEO of the Harrison Hunt Foundation."

"Really?" Deanna Steele said. "And you like working for the foundation?" There was just the faintest hint of surprise in her tone.

"It's all I've ever wanted to do."

She nodded, and he wondered what she was thinking.

"You don't have a drink," Terrence said, saving him from further questions. "C'mon, I'll show you where the bar is."

"I can do that, Daddy," Julie said.

"Now, sweetheart, you have other guests to attend to," Terrence said. "I'll take care of Alex."

Alex realized Terrence wanted to talk to him, so he gave Julie a smile and said, "I'll be right back."

Terrence put his arm around Alex's shoulder. "We set up the bar in the cabana."

Once they were out of earshot of Julie and Lucinda, Terrence said, "I'm going to have to make a trip to Singapore next week, Alex. Be gone about ten days."

Terrence was in the import/export business and frequently traveled abroad, especially to the Orient.

"I was hoping you'd keep an eye on the girls for me."

"Oh?" This was a first. "Something I should know?"

"It's not a big deal, just…" His voice trailed off.

By now they'd reached the bar and Alex ordered a vodka and tonic. Terrence waited until he'd got his drink and they'd moved away before saying anything else.

"Look," he said, leading Alex toward the back of the cabana where it was relatively quiet and no one else could hear their conversation. "Julie's been acting funny the past couple of weeks. I'm worried that maybe she's messing with drugs."

Jesus, Alex thought. "Have you said anything to her?"

Terrence shook his head. "I don't want to accuse her of something that might not be true."

"I'm not afraid to. I'll talk to her."

"It's not that I'm *afraid* to," Terrence protested. "I just…I trust my little girl."

*Then why the hell are you asking me to keep an eye on her?* Alex wondered if Terrence had any idea how contradictory he sounded. "Even sensible people can be led astray by the wrong kinds of friends."

"Her friends all come from the best families," Terrence blustered.

Alex raised his eyebrows.

Terrence had the grace to look sheepish. "I know, I know. That doesn't mean they can't get into trouble."

"No, it doesn't." Alex sipped at his

drink thoughtfully. It would be hard to keep an eye on Julie now that he was working in Jansen, which wasn't exactly close to the Queen Anne area where Julie lived with her parents. "I'm in the middle of a big project right now that's keeping me out of town most of the time, but one way or another, I'll keep tabs on Julie."

Terrence huffed a breath. "Thanks, Alex. I really appreciate that."

"I love Julie, too," Alex pointed out. "And I don't want her to get into trouble...or hurt herself."

"I know."

Alex made himself a promise as he and Terrence moved to rejoin the others. He would not only keep tabs on his sister, he would sit her down and talk to her.

In fact, he'd start tonight.


P.J. couldn't believe how disappointed she was that Alex hadn't shown up at Jake's. She wished she could ask Rick why, but of course, she couldn't.

She wondered if he was seeing someone. If maybe he had a date tonight. The thought bothered her a lot more than it should have.

*It's just your ego that's smarting. You were sure he was interested in you, and obviously, since he hasn't made a move to ask you out, he's not.*

*You should be glad. You've dodged a bullet. This is the best thing that could have happened...or not happened. Considering you've decided there was nowhere for a relationship with Alex to go, anyway.*

Yet no matter how many times she told herself all of this, she couldn't stop wondering where he was tonight.

And with whom.

It was nearly eleven before Julie opened her gifts, and by then Alex knew it was going to be impossible to talk to her that night. Resigned, he watched her indulgently as she squealed and exclaimed over each offering. He'd say one thing for her. She might be spoiled and pampered, but she wasn't jaded. He smiled wryly, remembering the Lotus. Well, maybe not totally.

"Oh, Alex, they're *gorgeous!*" she said upon seeing the tourmaline-set silver bracelet and earrings he'd given her. Coming over to where he stood, she kissed him. "Thank you," she said softly. "You always know what I'll love."

Love for her warmed him. Funny how she had so easily crept into his heart whereas he had always felt an off-putting distance with his brothers. Not for the first time, he wondered why that should be so. Perhaps it was being raised by a succession of nannies and the impersonal atmosphere of Harry's mansion. Or maybe it was simply Harry himself, so absorbed in his business and his money that he couldn't give much face time to his sons.

After Julie finished opening her gifts, Alex pulled her aside.

"I'm beat," he said. "I'm going to head out."

"You're *such* a party-pooper," she said, pouting. "We're all going to Twist, and

Phoebe's going to be *so* disappointed if you don't go with us."

"You know how I feel about the club scene."

Julie just shook her head. "Twist isn't a club. It's fun. You'd like it."

Alex smiled. "I've been there. I'll pass."

"Honestly, you'd think you were ninety instead of just thirty-six. You keep saying you're not stodgy, but I'm having a hard time believing it."

Alex shrugged. "Actually, I was hoping we could get together for a while tomorrow. There's something I want to talk to you about."

Julie frowned. "You sound serious. What's up?"

"I'd rather not get into it tonight. How about having lunch with me tomorrow?"

"Just as long as it's not too early. I'm not like you. I don't turn into a pumpkin at the stroke of midnight."

"Some of us *do* work for a living," he said mildly.

"Tomorrow's Sunday."

"You know what I meant."

They made arrangements to meet at a small seafood restaurant Alex liked that wasn't too far from the house. Alex suggested one o'clock, hopefully ensuring that Julie might be on time. Then he said his goodnights to everyone and headed back to Jansen.

The next day, promptly at one, Alex walked into the restaurant and secured a window table for two. As he'd expected, Julie hadn't made an appearance yet.

Alex ordered a glass of iced tea and the seafood appetizer the restaurant was known for—cold shrimp and crab in a spicy cocktail sauce—and settled in to wait.

Twenty minutes later, he had eaten most of the appetizer, and Julie still hadn't shown up. Sighing, he whipped out his cell phone and hit the speed dial number for her cell.

"I know, I know," she said when she answered. "Sorry. I slept through the alarm—I didn't get home till almost dawn—but I'm on my way now. I'll be there in ten."

Alex just shook his head. It was pointless to be angry with her. Since he knew she was always late, he should have just waited and arrived thirty minutes later himself.

When she walked in—as promised, ten minutes later—he marveled at how fresh and pretty she looked. That was the advantage of being young. Late hours didn't start to show until you were a lot older. Wearing a bright-yellow dress, long hair gleaming in the sunlight-filled restaurant, she resembled a younger version of Catherine Zeta Jones and drew admiring glances from the other diners. One man sitting alone at the bar stared at her so intently Alex was certain he was going to get up and try to talk to her. In fact, he leaned forward, putting one foot on the floor. But when Julie headed for Alex's table, waving and giving him a wide smile, the man relaxed back in his seat again.

Alex stood to greet her, giving her a kiss on the cheek.

"This has got to be a record," she said, "seeing you two days in a row." Her perfume, something light and flowery, drifted around him.

He pulled her chair out and she sank gracefully into it.

"You look awfully pretty today," he said, sitting again himself. "Hard to believe you got so little sleep."

She took her napkin out of her water glass and put it on her lap. "Thank you. Now that I've reached the ripe old age of twenty-two, I'm trying to take better care of myself."

Alex couldn't have hoped for a better opening. "Funny you should say that, because that's what I want to talk to you about."

Something in his expression or tone must have alerted her to the fact this might be a discussion she wouldn't enjoy, because she frowned.

Just then their waiter approached, so Alex didn't continue.

After she'd ordered something to drink, the waiter left them to study their menus.

"Well?" Julie said. "Are you going to tell me what's going on or am I going to have to guess?"

"Why don't we decide what we want to eat first? Otherwise we'll keep getting interrupted."

She looked as if she wanted to protest, but finally she just sighed and picked up her menu.

After placing their orders—Alex opted for the fried scallops, his favorite, and Julie ordered the crab quiche—Alex leaned forward and said, "Terrence talked to me last night. He's worried about you."

"Why?"

"He's concerned that you might be involved with drugs."

*"What?"* She looked aghast.

Alex studied her. Julie was a good actress, but he didn't think her reaction was fake. She looked genuinely shocked.

"Geez," she said. "You'd think he'd

know me a little better than that. I know why he thinks this, Alex, but he's wrong."

"Why does he think it?"

"Because Penn—you met him last night, the really tall one with the sort of reddish hair?—was busted at a party where they were doing coke. But I don't do drugs. I never have. They scare me."

Alex felt tremendous relief. Her voice rang with conviction, and he believed her. "I'm really glad to hear that."

"Did you really think I might be involved in that scene?"

"I didn't know what to think. I only knew that Terrence is concerned enough to ask me to keep an eye on you while he's gone."

"Where's he going now?"

"Singapore. Didn't he tell you?"

She shrugged. "He might have. He travels so much, I lose track of what he's doing."

She stopped talking as their waiter appeared with their food.

Once he left them alone again, Alex said, "What happened with your friend Penn?"

"What do you mean?"

"Was he charged? You said he was busted." He forked one of his scallops.

She grimaced. "Yes, he was charged with possession."

"And what happened?"

"I don't know. His dad's pulling some strings, I think. You know his dad, actually. Senator Pennbridge?" She ate some of her quiche.

Alex just shook his head. Why should that information surprise him? It happened too often, in his opinion. Kids with rich parents rarely paid the price for their foolish or unlawful behavior.

"I'd feel better if you didn't run around with him anymore."

Julie put her fork down and drank some of her iced tea. "But Alex, he's my friend. I like him."

"He sounds like a bad influence to me."

"He's learned his lesson. That bust scared the hell out of him." Picking up her fork, she resumed eating.

"For now maybe," Alex said skeptically.

"I told you. I don't do drugs. Now will you quit worrying? And will you tell Dad to quit worrying, too? I'm not a child. I don't need a keeper."

Alex figured he knew how parents must feel when their kids got older and they couldn't supervise their every moment as they did when they were little. You just had to trust that you'd taught them right and they'd be okay. Julie might be spoiled, but she was basically a good girl. She'd probably be just fine. Anyway, what choice did he have but to trust her?

As if she'd read his thoughts, she smiled and said, "Now, c'mon, Alex, quit looking so serious and let's enjoy our food."

Alex had always known when to fold. Returning his sister's smile, he nodded and turned his attention to his lunch.

Normally, P.J. really enjoyed her weekends, but for some reason, this weekend she felt restless.

She did her laundry, cleaned her condo then took a long, leisurely bath and washed her hair. These activities should have made her feel virtuous and proud of herself. Instead, they left her wishing she had somewhere to go, something fun to do and someone to do it with.

Here she was, thirty years old, single, and with nothing better to do on a Saturday night except watch a movie on DVD and order in a pizza. She'd be willing to bet Carrie Wancheck wasn't sitting home alone tonight. Or Alex, either.

Now why had she thought of those two, practically in the same breath?

*Oh, you know why.*

Was it possible that Carrie had accomplished her mission of catching Alex's interest? She hadn't been at Jake's the night before, either, and when P.J. had casually asked about her, one of the guys said Carrie had bragged that she had a hot date. *A sleep-over date,* he'd said, and the others had all laughed knowingly.

What if that hot date had been with Alex? Although it was the last thing she wanted to think about, P.J. couldn't help imagining the two of them in bed together. Carrie had a fantastic body—toned and slender, with curves in all the right places. What man wouldn't desire her?

The idea of the two of them together made P.J. want to throw up. And that made her even more disgusted with herself. Why did she care anyway? *You don't want him. So what's the problem?*

But even as she told herself this, P.J. knew exactly what the problem was. She *did* want him. And unfortunately, what she'd imagined to be a corresponding interest from him had turned out to be just plain normal friendliness on his part. Because if he'd been going to make a move in her direction, he'd darned sure have done it by now.

Really disgusted with herself now, she decided that once and for all, she would wipe Alex Noble out of her mind. Not only that, she would stay away from him at work as well as after work. If that meant she would have to give up going to Jake's, so be it. She needed some new interests in life, anyway. In fact, instead of just giving lip service to some of the areas that interested her, it was past time to put some of those interests into action. Like volunteering at a women's shelter. And getting involved in politics.

It was a good thing she had that management meeting in Seattle this week. She needed to get away. Maybe after a week of meetings, she'd have her head back in the game again.

And nowhere near Alex Noble.

## *Chapter Eight*

The week went fast for Alex. They were extremely busy at work, and it felt as if he'd no sooner had lunch than it would be time to punch out.

After work, he always ran his five miles in Jansen Park. He kept hoping he'd see P.J. there since Chick Fogarty had told them she was in management meetings in Seattle this week. But she didn't come to the park, or if she did, she came earlier or later than he did.

Because he was curious, he gave Gray a call and found out the meetings would be over by noon on Thursday. While he had Gray on the phone, he asked him how his bride hunt was going. As always, Gray was noncommittal.

"What about you?" he asked.

"I'm working on it," Alex said.

After they'd hung up, Alex wondered if P.J. would be back to work on Friday. He hoped so. Now that he'd decided Miss Paige Jeffers Kinkaid was the perfect candidate for his bride hunt, he was determined to make some forward progress in his campaign to win her.

On Friday morning, as he entered the quad, the first person he saw was P.J. sitting at her desk. She looked up when she heard his footsteps. "Good morning."

"Good morning," he said, smiling down at her. She looked great in a short-sleeved sweater the same blue as her eyes. It hugged her breasts and Alex couldn't help noticing the faint outline of her bra. "How were your meetings?"

She shrugged, not meeting his gaze. "Fine."

Alex started to say something else, but she'd already turned her attention back to her computer.

Alex frowned as he walked away. She certainly wasn't very friendly this morning. He wondered if something was wrong. And if so, if it had to do with him. Could she have found out who *he* was? But he didn't have time to think about her for long because only minutes later the morning orders began pouring in.

Again, the day went by fast. He barely saw P.J. When he passed her desk, she always seemed to be somewhere else, and she wasn't around at lunchtime, either. And when he did see her, she never stopped to talk, not even for a few minutes. By the end of the day, he had the distinct feeling she was purposely avoiding him.

When Rick asked if he was planning to go to Jake's after work, Alex said yes. He hoped P.J. would be there, too. If she was, he was going to make it his business to talk to her.

She was still at her desk when he and Rick left, and Alex was glad when Rick said, "Hey, boss, you goin' to Jake's?"

She looked up. Her gaze met Alex's for an instant before resting on Rick. After hesitating a moment, she shrugged. "I don't know."

"Ah, c'mon, boss," Rick cajoled. "Do you good to go. You've been uptight all day. Those meetings must've done you in. We'll see you there, okay?"

Alex wondered if she'd show up. He'd almost given up after an hour went by and she didn't appear. And then suddenly, there she was. She looked tired, not her usual lively self at all. Something must be wrong. Maybe whatever it was had nothing to do with Alex at all. Maybe the week had just been a rough one for her. He wished there was an empty chair near where he was sitting, but even though he'd tried to sit at the far end of the table where there was room for a few more, Rick wouldn't hear of it and had insisted Alex come and join him and Wayne and Jim, who were all sitting together.

The good thing was, Carrie Wancheck wasn't there. In fact, the only female to join the group that night was Ruby.

P.J. walked over to the bar, got herself a beer, then sat at the far end where Alex had initially wanted to sit, too.

Damn. She hadn't even acknowledged his presence, just gave a nod and general "hello" to everyone. Soon she was engaged in a conversation with Buddy Willis, one of the pickers from Quad A. Alex might have been worried at the intimate way they were talking, but Buddy couldn't have been more than twenty, way too young for P.J. After a few minutes, Ruby drifted down to that end of the table and joined them.

Rick nudged Alex. "Ruby's got the hots for Buddy."

Alex smiled. "What about him?"

Rick grinned. "I think he's into her, too."

About six, Rick said he had to go. Soon after that, the other married men left one by one. By six-thirty, only Alex, two of the dock workers, Buddy, Ruby and P.J. were left and finally Alex was close enough to P.J. to actually talk to her.

"While you were gone we had a really busy week," he said.

"I noticed."

"We missed you, though." He nudged Ruby. "Didn't we?"

Ruby grinned. "You might have. I didn't."

P.J. laughed. "Ruby tells it like it is."

"No, seriously, boss, we *did* miss you," Ruby said. "Things never go as smooth when you're not there."

"You don't have to flatter me," P.J. said. "I'm planning to give you a raise."

Ruby squealed. *"Really?"*

By now the two dock workers had decided they were ready to eat and waved the waitress over. Alex waited to see if P.J. was going to order, saw that she was, and placed his own order for a cheeseburger and fries.

After the waitress left to turn in the food orders, the two dock workers got up to play a game of darts. Alex wished Ruby and Buddy would find something to do so he could have P.J. to himself, but they sat there and dominated the conversation, which now centered on video games. At one point when they were arguing the merits of two different war-type games, Alex caught P.J.'s eye and he could see she was as bored as he was. He winked, and for the first time that day, he got a smile.

Once the food came, and the two dock workers returned to the table, the talk turned to the less-than-stellar season the Mariners were having.

"Damn games are too expensive," one of the dock workers grumbled. "Pretty soon only rich people will be able to afford big-league sports."

Alex felt a guilty pang at the thought of the HuntCom sky box. He could go to a game any time he wished and sit in comfort, yet he rarely went. He made a mental note that when this charade of his was over, he would invite some of his co-workers from the distribution center to a game or two.

After they'd eaten, the dock workers got up to play another game of darts and Ruby and Buddy decided to have a game of pool.

"Well," P.J. said after they'd left the table, "I really should be going."

"Me, too," Alex said, although he had no reason to leave. But if she was going, he also had no reason to stay.

They paid their tabs, said goodbye to the others, and walked outside together. The late September evening had already cooled considerably, and P.J. shivered. Alex wished he'd worn a jacket. He'd have given it to her.

"Where's your car?" he asked.

She pointed to far end of the parking lot.

"I'll walk down there with you," he said.

"It's not necessary—" she began.

"I know, but I'll come anyway."

When they reached the car, she went to

the driver's side, pausing before inserting her key. "Have a good weekend."

Alex didn't intend to let another weekend go by without asking her out. "Wait, P.J.," he said as she started to unlock the door.

She looked up. It wasn't completely dark yet, and in the half light of dusk, it was hard to read her expression.

"I was wondering…if you're not busy tomorrow night…would you like to have dinner with me?"

"I…" She licked her lips. "Thank you, but I don't think so."

Alex had not expected her to say no. For a moment, he stood there awkwardly. Faint sounds of music came from inside Jake's, and somewhere nearby a car back-fired.

"Look, Alex, I really like you, and I'm flattered you asked, but I just don't think it's a good idea to date someone who works for me."

*Damn.* He hadn't even thought of that. She was right. In normal circumstances, it *wasn't* a good idea. Of course, their circumstances were far from normal. The fact that he wasn't who he was pretending to be was something she couldn't know. And she certainly had no idea he knew *her* real background.

"I hope you understand," she said.

What could he say? "Sure, I understand."

How was he going to get around *this* obstacle? he wondered. Maybe he couldn't. Maybe he'd have to find someone else to fulfill Harry's challenge. But dammit, he didn't want to.

When P.J. got into her car, Alex waved and walked toward his truck. He was just unlocking it when he heard the whine of her starter. The sound was unmistakable. Her car wouldn't start.

Hurriedly, he got into his truck, started it and drove down to where she still sat futilely trying to get the Miata's engine to catch.

He set the brake, then climbed out of the truck and walked to her side of the car. She lowered the window.

"I'll give you a jump," he said.

"You have cables with you?"

"Yep. I was a Boy Scout."

"Be prepared," she said, smiling.

Her car started on the first try.

"Let it run a few minutes. Then I'll take the cables off," he said. Once he was sure her car wasn't going to die on her, he unhooked the cables and lowered her hood. "I'll follow you home, make sure you get there okay."

"Oh, Alex, that's totally unnecessary," she said. "I'll be fine."

"I'll follow you." His tone left no room for argument.

"All right. Thank you."

She lived fairly close to Alex's apartment complex. When they reached her building she put her window down and when he pulled up next to her said, "Would you like to come in for coffee or a glass of wine?"

"Sounds good." Which was an understatement.

"You can park in one of the visitor slots in front," she said. "I'm going to go park in back. My unit is 112."

Alex parked the truck, found unit 112, which was located at the far end, and sat on the low stone wall bordering the front walkway. He wondered why she had invited him to come in. He'd have thought after refusing his invitation to go out with him, she would simply have thanked him and said goodnight.

A few minutes later, her front door opened. She smiled, standing back to let him in. When she closed the door, she leaned back against it, and their eyes met. For a long moment, their gazes held. Without conscious thought, Alex reached for her. There was no hesitation on her part. As if she, too, knew there was no use fighting what they both were feeling, she simply stepped into his arms and raised her lips to meet his.

P.J.'s head spun as the kiss went on and on. Part of her, the tiny part that was still capable of rational thought, was shouting, *What are you doing? This is madness!* But the rest of her, oh, the rest of her, was reveling in the thrilling sensations flooding her body. Desire, something she hadn't felt in a long time, ignited every inch of her flesh.

One kiss became two, two became three. Soon kissing wasn't enough. She wanted more.

And more.

When Alex's hands slid under her sweater she shivered. When they found her breasts, she moaned. When he unhooked her bra, she never said stop. When he raised her sweater to get it off, she finished the job herself.

Then she reached for his belt buckle. The only sounds in the room were the ticking of the grandfather clock that had belonged to her grandmother Marjorie, the muted hum of traffic from the highway nearby, and their frenzied lovemaking.

They never even made it to the bedroom, which was both a good and a bad thing. The good thing was she stopped thinking and just let delicious sensation take over.

The bad thing was she stopped thinking and just let delicious sensation take over. It had been a long time since she'd felt this way.

Maybe she'd *never* felt this way.

Later, she never remembered exactly what happened. She only knew that her clothes ended up scattered over the floor along with his, that they didn't even seek the relative comfort of the couch but fell to the carpet.

Alex touched her and kissed her, finding every hidden place that yearned to be touched and kissed. And just at the point where P.J. thought she could stand it no longer, he thrust into her, pushing deep and hard, then deeper still. She reveled in the heat of him and cried out again and again as she crescendoed to a climax, and seconds later, he buried his face in her neck and muffled his own cry as he shuddered with his own release.

Afterwards, they lay twined together as their hearts gradually slowed.

It was only then that sanity returned.

P.J. sat up. Spying her sweater she grabbed it and put it on. She didn't look at Alex. Couldn't. What must he think of her? She'd been wanton tonight.

"P.J." he said softly. He caressed her arm. "You're not sorry, are you?"

*Oh, God.*

"Because I'm not."

*Of course not. You're a man. You have nothing to lose.*

"I'm…only sorry about not having a condom. Truth is, I never even thought about a condom. I didn't think about anything…except you." Taking her hand, he turned it palm up and kissed it.

P.J. shivered and finally turned to look at him. Her heart thudded as their gazes met. She forced herself to keep her eyes trained on his face instead of sweeping down his magnificent body.

And it *was* magnificent.

Alex Noble was one of the finest male specimens she'd ever seen. Just thinking about how fine he was made her want him all over again.

"Don't worry," she forced herself to say in as normal a voice as possible. "I'm on birth control pills." The moment the lie was out of her mouth, she was sorry she'd said it. But what *should* she have said? *Don't worry, Alex. I probably couldn't get pregnant if I tried, because my insides are totally screwed up. So you're safe.*

Sure, the doctors had said there was a slim—very slim—chance she might be able to conceive, but they hadn't held out much hope. In fact, the last specialist she'd seen had said in all honesty he would put her chances at about ten percent, if that. And the older she got, the slimmer that percentage became.

At any rate, she had no intention of discussing her health issues with Alex…or any man, for that matter. After all, it wasn't as if he'd asked her to marry him. All they'd done was have great sex.

*You just keep telling yourself that, P.J.*

"That's good," Alex said. "But I wanted you to know that I believe in safe sex."

Hell's bells, she hadn't even thought of

that. *Of course not. You weren't thinking, period.*

Seeing the look on her face, he said, "I'm clean. I promise you. You're in no danger."

She nodded.

"I wish you'd say something." Leaning over, he kissed her cheek, then nuzzled her ear.

Oh, God. If she didn't get up and away from him, she'd succumb again, she knew she would. She could already feel herself weakening. "What do you want me to say?" Even her voice sounded weak. What in the world was wrong with her? She never let a man get the upper hand. But here she was acting like some kid with her first big crush instead of a thirty-year-old, experienced, fully independent woman who should know better.

"Say you'll go out with me tomorrow night," he said softly. His hand inched up under her sweater again, finding her bare breasts. When his thumb rubbed the nub of the one closest to him, P.J. fought with herself for all of about three seconds, then relaxed into him and turned her face for his kiss.

A long time later…a *very* long time later…after the most satisfying and wonderful sex P.J. could ever have imagined, she finally lay sated and resigned to her fate. She knew what she was doing was crazy and stupid. She knew one of these days she'd be very sorry and probably have to pay a price for her lapse in judgment. But at that moment, she really didn't care.

"So what do you say? Is it a date?" Alex asked lazily.

"Yes," P.J. said. She could feel his smile, even though she didn't look at him.

"I'll pick you up at seven."

"Okay."

"And P.J.?"

Sighing, she finally turned her head to meet his eyes.

He smiled. "Wear something sexy. You *do* own a dress?"

For just a second, P.J. bristled. Then she

grinned. "I've got a dress that'll knock your socks off."

"I can hardly wait."


Alex whistled all the way home.

P.J. was incredible. Somehow he'd suspected she would be. But suspecting and actually experiencing *how* incredible were two distinctly different things.

He smiled, remembering.

Yes. P.J. Kinkaid, alias Paige Jeffers Kinkaid, heiress to a fortune, who obviously believed in working for a living, was the perfect candidate for his Cinderella. Beautiful, smart, sexy, generous, kind and passionate.

What more could he want?


Courtney gave P.J. a quizzical smile. "Okay, spill. What's going on?"

At P.J.'s request, the sisters had met for coffee at a Starbucks near where Courtney lived.

P.J. drank some of her latte before answering. "Remember the new guy who came to work for me? The one I told you about when we had dinner together three weeks ago?"

Courtney grinned and broke off a piece of her muffin. "I knew this had to be about a man."

P.J. blew out a breath. "I don't know what to do."

"About what? Has he asked you out?"

"Yes, but that's not it."

Courtney stared at her. Lowering her voice, she said, "Uh-oh. You've done it, haven't you?"

P.J. didn't even pretend not to understand. Glumly, she nodded.

"What's wrong? Was it awful?"

"No, just the opposite, in fact. It…it was fantastic."

Courtney sighed and ate some of her muffin. "You lucky dog. Tell me everything."

So P.J. did, starting with how she'd tried to ignore Alex and ending with how they'd had sex. Twice. "On the *floor*, no less!" she said in a fierce whisper.

Courtney sighed again. "Sounds absolutely wonderful to me." Her voice was wistful. "I can remember when Brad and I used to have unplanned, sweaty and wonderful sex. That was sans kids, of course."

Sans kids. *I'll always be sans kids.* For some reason, the thought hurt. Really hurt. That surprised P.J. She'd thought she was long past the pain of knowing she would probably never have a child of her own.

"So what now? Are you in love with him?" Courtney asked eagerly.

"I don't know how I feel. I'm certainly in lust with him."

"Well, that's a good start. Are you seeing him again?"

P.J. nodded. "Tonight."

"Is he taking you out or are you just going to cut to the chase?"

"We're having dinner together. But I was halfway thinking I should call him and cancel."

*"What?* Why?"

"For all the reasons I gave you before.

Number one, this relationship can't go anywhere. And number two, he works for me."

"Wait a minute…why can't it go anywhere?"

"You know why…marriage is not for me."

"So? You can just live together. And as far as the job thing goes, find another job. Jobs are a dime a dozen. But trust me on this, Paige. Great guys are hard to find. No, not hard. *Impossible!*"

P.J. stared at her sister as though she'd lost her mind. "Quit my *job?*"

"I would. Shoot, P.J., if you've found someone special and he could be 'the one' what's a job compared to that? Besides, you and I both know you don't need to work." She finished off the last bite of her muffin and wiped her mouth with her napkin.

"I *like* working."

"Okay, fine. You like working. But it doesn't have to be there, does it? Dad can set you up with any kind of job you want."

"I don't want any favors from Dad."

Courtney rolled her eyes. "You are the most stubborn person I've ever known. Dad would love to have you working for him."

P.J. was sure her sister was right. But she'd put in more than seven years at HuntCom. She was respected there, not for being the daughter of the owner as she would be at one of her father's facilities, but for her intelligence and hard work. She didn't want to leave HuntCom. "There's something else…" she finally said.

"What?"

"I don't really know anything about Alex."

"Like what?"

"Well…he obviously comes from a classy background. So why is he working a blue-collar job? He's got to be hiding something."

"Paige, listen to you. *You're* hiding something."

P.J. frowned. "I know, but I have a

damned good reason. I don't want to be treated differently than my coworkers, and they *would* treat me differently if they knew about the Kincaid money."

"So? Maybe *he* has a damned good reason, too."

"What if he's hiding something bad?"

"Like what?" Courtney said again.

"I don't know. I just—" She broke off. "Something doesn't seem quite right with him."

"Have you asked him why he's working there?"

"Yes."

"What did he say?"

"He admitted he'd gone to college but didn't like the business world."

"P.J., this guy sounds perfect. In fact, he sounds just like you!"

P.J. made a face. "I'm not sure he told me the truth."

"But…what other reason could he have for doing the kind of work he's doing?"

"He could be a spy."

"A spy!"

"Yeah, a spy. Corporate spies exist, you know."

"Do you really think that?"

"I don't know." The truth was, P.J. didn't know *what* she thought. "I Googled him, you know."

Courtney smiled. "And?"

"Nothing. Well, there were Alex Nobles, but none that matched him."

"That doesn't mean anything."

"I know, but still…"

"You want to know what I think?"

P.J. nodded.

"I think you're scared."

P.J. wanted to deny this, but she had a sinking feeling her sister was right. The truth was, Alex was dangerous to her well-being. It was as if he'd gotten into her brain and rewired it or something. Hadn't last night proven that? Just being near him had messed with her mind to the extent she'd behaved in a way she'd never have imagined herself doing.

Courtney drained her latte and stood up. "I've got to go. But I have one last thing to say. If you push Alex away because you're scared, then you're not the woman I thought you were."

And with that, she blew P.J. a kiss, and walked out of the coffee shop.

## Chapter Nine

Alex decided to go for broke. After doing a bit of research, he called and made a reservation at the River Lodge, which stood on a rise overlooking the Jansen River a few miles north of town. Supposedly, the Lodge was one of the nicest restaurants around and famous for its great seafood and tender steaks. And on Friday and Saturday nights, a combo played live music. It sounded perfect and romantic, just what he wanted. After all, he didn't have a lot of time to woo P.J. Harry's deadline was only nine months away.

Alex also made the round trip into downtown Seattle and unearthed one of his favorite outfits: custom-made dress pants in a shade of soft gray, a dark gray silk T-shirt, and a black cashmere jacket. The clothes were expensive, but if she happened to comment, he could sheepishly admit that he occasionally splurged on good clothes.

On the way back to Jansen, he stopped at a florist's shop. The florist—a pretty woman about fifty with bright green eyes—asked if she could help him.

"I'd like a bouquet of flowers. Roses, probably."

"For a woman?"

"A special woman," Alex said.

"What color is her hair?"

Alex blinked. "Her hair? It's red. Actually, kind of a red-gold."

"Then I suggest peach roses." So saying, she walked to a large cooler and removed a container.

The moment Alex saw the color, he knew they were perfect.

"Have a wonderful evening," the florist said after Alex had paid for the flowers and was leaving.

"I intend to," he said, smiling.

He left his apartment at six-forty-five and arrived at her condo ten minutes later. The florist had talked him into letting her put the flowers in a vase instead of taking them to P.J. in a box. "You'll be glad you did," she'd said. "Otherwise, your special lady will have to find somewhere to put them and she might not have a tall enough vase."

Holding the vase in one hand, Alex rang P.J.'s doorbell with the other. She opened the door on the second ring.

*Holy cow.* He was stunned by how she looked. She wore a short black sleeveless dress with a high neck, paired with strappy black heels. Her curly hair was swept back and held in place by a black velvet hair band, and diamond studs sparkled in her ears.

Gorgeous.

There was no other word for it. She looked gorgeous.

"Wow," he said.

She smiled. "I clean up good, huh?"

"That's an understatement."

She stood back to let him in. "So do you." She gave him an appreciative once-over. "Nice threads."

"Thanks." He handed her the flowers. "I hope you like roses."

"I love roses, and these are just beautiful. Thank you."

He could see her pleasure was genuine, and it made him feel good. He tried to remember the last time he'd spontaneously bought flowers for a woman and couldn't. In fact, he couldn't remember the last time he'd looked forward to being with a woman. Most of his social life consisted of obligatory attendance at some black-tie affair.

When she turned to place the vase on the small credenza in her entryway, Alex's breath stopped for a moment. Her dress plunged in a deep V in the back—almost to her waist—exposing smooth porcelain skin. Skin he knew would warm to his touch.

He could feel himself becoming aroused and had to force his thoughts away from that skin and how it had felt last night. "You'll need a wrap," he said. "It's already cooling off."

"I know." She reached for a black knit shawl lying on a needlepoint-covered chair next to the credenza and wrapped it around her shoulders. Picking up a small silk bag that had been under it, she gave him a bright smile. "I'm ready."

As they walked out into the already darkening evening, Alex could smell her perfume—something light and clean— just the kind of fragrance he would have imagined she'd wear. When they reached his truck, he helped her in. Her legs looked fantastic in those heels. He wondered if she knew how fantastic. "I'm sorry I don't have a nice car for the occasion."

"I like trucks," she said with a smile.

"Hey, what happened with your car?" he asked after he had walked around and gotten into the driver's seat.

"My neighbor gave me a jump this morning, and I took it to Sears for a new battery."

"Good."

She shifted in the seat, which caused her skirt to ride up another inch or so. Yes, those were definitely gorgeous legs. In fact, he was having a hard time keeping his eyes on the road.

"Where are we going?" she asked.

He smiled. "It's a surprise." Turning to her, he added, "Want to listen to music?"

"What're my choices?"

He thought about his CDs. "Sheryl Crow, Martina McBride, Michelle Branch, Beyoncé, James Taylor, the Beatles, Coldplay…I've even got some classical stuff, if you prefer that."

She started to laugh. "That's the strangest mix of music I've ever heard."

He grinned sheepishly. "I've got eclectic tastes."

"I *guess*."

"So what'll it be?"

"Martina McBride."

He inserted the CD. The first song was "My Baby Loves Me," and within moments, P.J. was tapping her fingers on the console between the front seats and humming along with the music. When the song ended and the next one began, she said, "We're going to the River Lodge, aren't we?"

"Yes."

He could feel her eyes on him. Turning to meet her gaze, he saw the speculative look. "What?" he said.

"You're just full of surprises, aren't you? How'd you know about the Lodge?"

"The Internet. I just searched on restaurants and that one seemed to fill the bill." Now he wondered if he'd made a mistake. He couldn't afford to make her suspicious again, now that she seemed to finally trust him. First he needed to get a ring on her finger. "I wanted to take you somewhere nice."

"The Lodge is very nice," she said softly. "I haven't been there in a long time."

It suddenly hit him how much he wanted to please this woman…and keep pleasing her. Maybe his father's plan was unorthodox, but it sure seemed to be working. This was the first time in years—maybe the first time ever—that Alex had felt this way about a woman. Usually, he was counting the minutes until he could escape.

"The drive is coming up right around this bend," she said. "It'll be on your left." She smiled when he glanced her way. "It's kind of hard to see if you've never been there."

An understatement, Alex realized. On his own, he would have passed it up. Only a small sign marked the turn, and in the dark, it was almost impossible to see.

The drive climbed uphill for about one hundred yards, then turned to the left through a stand of tall pines. Finally they came to a rustic building surrounded by trees and bordering the Jansen River to the right. The trees were strung with tiny white lights and reminded Alex of Tavern on the Green in New York.

He surrendered the truck to the valet parking attendant and, hand on her elbow, escorted P.J. through the front entrance and into the restaurant. A pretty hostess with long black hair and a brilliant smile greeted them. Alex gave his name—almost saying *Hunt* before he caught himself—and they were promptly ushered to a table by the window. The river beyond was a dark ribbon with patches of moonlight shining upon it.

Alex looked around. He'd been in some high-end restaurants over the years, and the River Lodge compared favorably in ambiance. Now if the food lived up to its touted excellence, he'd be a happy man.

About thirty tables ringed a small dance floor. In the corner was a tiny elevated stage with a grand piano next to it. Either the combo providing music for the evening hadn't started yet or they were taking a break.

"The musicians start playing at eight," P.J. said.

A lighted candle flickered in a cut-glass holder in the middle of their table. Her face, reflected in the candle's glow, seemed younger and softer than it normally did. Maybe that's because she was more relaxed. She smiled at him. "This is nice."

"It is." He wished he could tell her about some of the places he'd been, some of the places he'd like to take her…but that would be too dangerous.

Just then their waiter approached, and the next few minutes were taken up with ordering drinks. After he left to place their orders at the bar, Alex said, "I've been looking forward to this all day."

She didn't answer for a long moment. When she did, she prefaced it with a sigh. "I don't know, Alex. I keep thinking this is a mistake."

"A mistake?" He couldn't have read her wrong. She'd been just as turned on last night as he'd been. She certainly hadn't resisted.

She met his gaze squarely. "You work for me. Remember?"

Reaching across the table, he took her hand. Her fingers were slim, the nails unpainted but nicely shaped. "I'll make you a promise, P.J. If my working for you turns out to be a problem, I'll find another job."

Before she could answer, their waiter arrived with their wine. Alex reluctantly let go of her hand. They didn't talk as the waiter served them a plate of some kind of pâté and a basket of warm French bread.

Once he was gone, she said, "I couldn't let you do that, Alex. It wouldn't be right." Worry clouded her blue eyes.

"Why don't you let me be the judge of that?" He reached for his wineglass. "Let's not have any more talk about anything serious. Let's just dedicate tonight, our first real date, to enjoying each other's company and having a wonderful time."

She hesitated, then picked up her glass and clinked it against his. But the worry didn't leave her eyes.

Alex vowed then and there that from

tonight on, he would make sure that worry was gone…and stayed gone.

There was something about dancing that was so sexy and erotic. If a girl felt even a smidgen of attraction for her partner, she was probably a lost cause once he took her into his arms and led her around a dance floor. And if the music was soft and romantic and the partner a great dancer—well, it was no contest.

P.J. knew that she and Alex would end up in bed together at the end of this perfect evening. She could tell herself whatever lie she wanted, but the bottom line was, her body would rule. In fact, sex with Alex was all she could think about as they danced and ate their superb dinners and drank the mellow wine.

By the time they were ready to leave, she was so turned on, she wasn't sure she could wait.

For the ride home, Alex unearthed a CD, and as the understated elegance of the singer's vocals filled the cab, the tension and delicious anticipation of what was to come pulsed like a living thing between them, and P.J. knew Alex was feeling exactly the same way she was.

When they reached P.J.'s condo, he parked in front and they walked together to her front door. The very air seemed to shimmer in expectation.

When Alex reached for her keys, she gave them up without a word. They stood so close, she wondered if he could hear her heart beating. After he unlocked the door and pushed it open, P.J. stepped inside knowing he would follow.

The small hurricane lamp on the credenza in the entryway gave off a soft glow, illuminating the roses in their frosted vase. Their fragrance filled the air. P.J. turned and their eyes met. As the grandfather clock began to chime the hour, he reached for her and pulled her close. When he lowered his head, she raised hers and gave herself up to his kiss.

A long time later, after making love, sleeping for a while, then waking and making love again, they lay together spoon fashion in P.J.'s bed.

"We fit together nicely," Alex said, lazily cupping a breast and nuzzling the back of her neck.

"Ummm," P.J. murmured noncommittally, although she'd been thinking the same thing.

"You're not going to let our work situation make a difference between us, are you?"

"Depends how things go." But she already knew she wouldn't. Because if she made their jobs an issue, she'd have to give him up, and she didn't want to. Of course, if it became a situation where she could no longer do her job or he could no longer do his, she'd have to rethink her decision.

But for now, at least, she intended to enjoy being with Alex…and not worry about tomorrow.

The next few weeks went by swiftly. Alex kept his promise to keep tabs on Julie, but was relieved when Terrence returned home from his business trip and Alex no longer felt quite as responsible for her.

He and P.J. spent a lot of time together. He took her to movies, they went out to dinner, they fell into the habit of running together after work, and one Saturday afternoon and evening they attended a festival at the local Catholic church.

"I love Ferris wheels," P.J. said as they stood in line waiting their turn to ride.

Alex smiled down at her. She looked like a kid in her jeans and flip-flops with her hair pulled back in a ponytail.

"I almost came to this festival last year," she continued.

"Why didn't you?"

She shrugged, the smile fading. "No one to go with."

The way she said it made Alex feel tender toward her. She acted so tough most of the time, but he suspected the toughness was a facade to mask deeper feelings.

*Maybe she's lonely, too.*

Most people, he'd discovered, presented

a face to the world that was not necessarily their real face. He certainly did. No one who knew him socially or in the world of philanthropy would ever guess at the emotions he kept hidden. Even his half-brothers probably had no idea what he was really like, just as he had little idea what made *them* tick.

"Well, you've got me now," he said, putting his arm around her.

Their eyes met, and Alex could tell she wanted to say something—was actually on the verge of saying something—but just then the line began to move and the moment was lost.

Later that night, Alex awakened to the sound of rain hitting the roof. P.J. was still sleeping soundly. He smiled as he watched her. She looked delectable. There was no other word for it. Her hair tumbled over the pillow, her sleep shirt—which she'd put back on after they'd made love—had ridden up, and her really gorgeous backside was visible. It was all he could do to keep from caressing it, but he knew if he did, he'd wake her. He resisted the temptation. They had all day tomorrow to enjoy each other. He was just drifting back to sleep when his cell phone rang. Groaning, he picked it up off the bedside table and looked at the caller ID.

*Julie.*

The digital clock on P.J.'s side of the bed read 4:43 a.m.

"Damn," he muttered, pressing talk and getting out of bed as quietly as he could. "This had better be important," he whispered, moving toward the hallway.

"Alex," Julie cried. "I've...I've been arrested!"

*"What?* Why?"

"I didn't *do* anything, but they won't listen to me. They hauled me down here to the police station just like a common criminal!"

"Calm down. *Why* were you arrested?"

"It was a drug raid. I—I was at Sandpipers and some of the kids were doing coke and stuff."

"Jesus, Julie." Alex pushed his hair back from his forehead in frustration.

"Well, I wasn't *part* of it. I was just *there*. They had no right to arrest me! Oh, God, I don't want Mom and Dad to know. Can you come?"

He sighed. "Yes, I'll come. Where, exactly, are you?"

After she told him, he said, "It'll be an hour, hour and a half before I get there."

"Okay," she said in a small voice. "Thank you, Alex."

By the time Alex had dressed and gathered his stuff, P.J. was stirring.

"You leaving already?" she said sleepily, sitting up in bed.

"I have to." He walked around to her side of the bed, leaned down, and kissed her. "I probably won't get back before noon."

Her brow furrowed. "Is something wrong?"

"I just got a call from my sister. I've got to drive to Seattle and bail her out of jail."

P.J.'s eyes widened. "What happened?"

"It was a drug bust at a club. Look, I've got to get going. I'll call you later, okay?"

She nodded. "Be careful driving."

He made it to the precinct where Julie was being held in record time, but even so, it was almost six-thirty before he walked in. It took another thirty minutes before he was allowed to see her.

She sat on a bench in a holding cell, along with a dozen other young people. Alex gritted his teeth when he recognized the infamous Penn, who sat with his head in his hands. He looked up when Alex and the duty cop approached. Alex nodded in the boy's direction, even as he wished he could pound some sense into him and the others. He did notice that the beautiful Phoebe wasn't part of the group. So, obviously, she was smarter than Julie.

"Alex," Julie said, getting up and coming toward him. Her mascara was smudged, her blouse wrinkled and dirty, her face pale and exhausted-looking. A lone tear rolled down her face as her blue eyes met Alex's.

Alex reached through the bars and took

her hand. The duty cop unlocked the cell and let Julie out.

"Fifteen minutes," he barked after taking them to a small, windowless room with a table and several chairs. "Then she's gotta go back till bail is set."

"When will that be?" Alex asked.

The cop made a show of looking up at the large, ugly wall clock. "Lemme see, it's seven-ten. Judge Winkle won't be in chambers till nine. So that means at least two hours, prob'ly more."

"Two more hours!" Julie said.

"Yeah, cutie. It's no fun here, is it?" With that the cop left them.

"Alex," she cried, the tears starting in earnest now.

He let her cry for a while. Just held her in his arms and rubbed her back and made comforting sounds. When she finally stopped, he handed her a clean handkerchief. "Sit down, Julie. Tell me what happened."

"I told you. We were just at Sandpipers and—"

"Who's we?"

"Me, Bits, Crystal, Logan, Phoebe—"

"Phoebe? I didn't see her back there," Alex said, interrupting her again.

Julie rolled her eyes. "She ran. The cops didn't see her, I guess."

"Who else was there?"

"Russ, Terri, and Penn. You met some of them at my birthday party."

"Penn's the one who was busted before for drugs. The one your dad was worried about. The one I told you to stay away from."

She hung her head. "Yes."

Alex sighed. "Hell, Julie, when are you ever going to learn?"

"But I wasn't doing anything. I was just there. It's so not fair. Couldn't they give me some kind of test or something? Did they have to arrest me?"

"Haven't you ever heard that old saying that you're known by the company you keep?"

The tears began again. "Daddy's going to kill me."

"He should, but I doubt he will."

"I don't want him to know. Please don't tell him. You won't, will you?"

"On one condition."

Her eyes, so big, so blue, so frightened, perpetuated the myth that she really was as naive and sweet as she appeared to be. But Alex knew better. Sure he loved her. And yes, he wanted to protect her, especially from her own bad judgment, but she was already too wise in the ways of the world and far too sophisticated and indulged for her own good. Right then he was torn between feeling sorry for her and wanting to turn her over his knee and give her the spanking she should have had many years ago.

"What's the condition?" she asked.

"You have to promise me nothing like this will ever happen again."

"It won't! I promise."

"Because if it does…" He paused to let his next words sink in. "I'm not going to come to the rescue."

She nodded solemnly. "I understand."

"I hope so."

A few minutes later, the same duty cop came back. He opened the door without knocking, said, "Time to go, Missy." His pale eyes met Alex's gaze. "You can wait out front."

It was almost ten o'clock before bail was set. By then Alex had drunk half a dozen cups of bad coffee and had a whale of a headache. The only good thing was that because this was a first offense for Julie, it only cost Alex a thousand dollars to get her released.

"Where's your car?" he said as they claimed her belongings—a leather shoulder bag and a black leather jacket.

"I didn't drive last night."

"Okay. I'll take you home."

As they walked out the front door into the morning sunshine, a photographer, who had been sitting on the concrete wall bordering the building, jumped up and snapped a couple of photos before Alex could react.

"Oh, God," Julie said. "Now Dad will find out for sure."

"Maybe you should just tell him yourself."

Julie, too miserable to be aware of anything except her own situation, slumped into the passenger seat of Alex's truck and never even asked why he was driving it instead of his Navigator.

"You want to stop and have some breakfast on the way?" Alex asked.

Julie shook her head. "I'm not hungry. Just pull into the drive through at the first Starbucks you see and get me a giant latte, okay?"

It was eleven-thirty before he finally dropped Julie at the house. She insisted he let her out at the foot of the drive so no one would see him. "They expected me to spend the night at Phoebe's," she said.

"Like I said, if I were you, I'd tell them the truth."

She nodded, leaned over and kissed his cheek. "Thanks, bro," she whispered.

"I'll call you later."

"Okay."

He watched until she disappeared

around the bend of the driveway, then took off.

It was only as he was driving back to Jansen that he remembered he hadn't called P.J. as he'd said he would. He flipped open his cell phone, ready to make the call, then wondered what he was going to say. Could he afford to tell her the whole truth?

Damn, he hated this subterfuge. Above all, he wished they could be completely honest with one another.

Soon, he thought. If things between them continued to go well in the next few weeks, he should be able to tell her the truth about himself by Thanksgiving.

And with luck, they might even be married by Christmas.

## Chapter Ten

After Alex left, P.J. tried to go back to sleep, but hadn't been able to. Finally, at five-thirty, she gave up, got up, showered, pulled on clean jeans and a warm sweater, then padded barefoot into the kitchen to make a pot of coffee. Peering out front, she saw that the Sunday newspaper had been delivered.

She slipped into an old pair of clogs and unlocked the front door. The early-morning air was crisp and cold after the night's storm, but it was supposed to warm up to the sixties this afternoon. She hoped the weatherman had been right. She and Alex had talked about going bike riding today, and it would be more pleasant if the weather was warmer.

She wondered if Alex would still want to go. She also wondered about his sister. Funny he had never mentioned her before. Of course, he hadn't talked about his family much at all. When asked, he'd said he had brothers who lived in the Seattle area and once, when she'd pressed a little, he'd said his parents were divorced. Although she'd been intensely curious to know more, she hadn't wanted to press too hard because he might press back, and she absolutely did *not* want to talk about her family if she could help it.

Oh, she'd told him she had two sisters and a brother and a total of seven nieces and nephews, but she'd changed the subject as soon as she could. Maybe one day she'd tell him about her family—who and what they were—but it was too soon.

And perhaps pointless. Whether or not she came clean with Alex about her background would depend on what developed with their relationship.

*Oh? And what happened to "this relationship can go nowhere?"*

P.J. purposely ignored the little voice inside her that persisted in reminding her just how naive she'd been. And yet, had she really? Hadn't she always known, down deep, that a casual relationship with Alex wasn't possible? From the beginning, she'd been far too attracted to him. In fact, he should have been wearing a sign that said Danger Ahead. *Oh, hell, Kincaid. He was wearing the sign. You just pretended not to see it.*

As the morning wore on, as P.J. fixed herself some scrambled eggs and toast, as she read the paper, as she tidied her condo, she kept looking at the phone and wondering where Alex was now and what he was doing. She wished he'd call as he'd promised. Didn't he realize she was concerned? Worried?

A little after one the phone finally rang. Dropping her magazine, she rushed to answer it.

"Still want to take that bike ride?" he asked.

"If you do."

"Good. I'll be there in fifteen minutes."

"Park in back, by the garage. Easier to load the bikes that way."

When he arrived, P.J. could see he'd stopped at his apartment to shower and change clothes before coming to her place. "Are you sure you still want to go?" she asked. "You look tired."

"I am, but I need the fresh air."

"Have you had any lunch?"

"I grabbed a sandwich at the apartment."

She was dying to ask about his sister, but something held her back. "Okay, then. Let's get the bikes."

Ten minutes later, bikes in the bed of the pickup, they headed out to the park. They'd briefly toyed with the idea of driving to the coast, maybe to Seaside, but decided the Jansen River trail was just as nice and a heckuva lot easier to get to. Plus Seaside on a beautiful Sunday afternoon was almost always crowded. And P.J. had learned early in their relationship that in this she and Alex were alike—neither enjoyed crowds. The carnival yesterday was enough for one weekend.

"This is nice," Alex said once they were comfortably into their ride along the river. He smiled at her. "Thanks for not asking about the morning."

"Just because I didn't ask doesn't mean I'm not curious."

"I want to tell you. I just wasn't in the mood to talk about it until now." He grimaced. "I hope that's my last encounter with the criminal justice system."

He then proceeded to explain what had happened.

"She must have been awfully scared," P.J. said when he was finished.

"Yes. I only hope it lasts. Julie has a tendency to forget about consequences when she's out raising hell." He sighed.

"The problem is, she's never had to take responsibility for anything. Someone always bails her out. Today I did the bailing."

P.J. knew he was as frustrated with himself as he was with his sister. "How old is Julie?"

"She just turned twenty-two."

"Has she been in any serious trouble before?" P.J. couldn't help but think about her own sister Jillian, who was a model citizen now, but who had been a wild child when she was young. Shoot, P.J. herself hadn't exactly been a model citizen. And she'd be extremely surprised if Alex had, either.

"Nothing too serious. She got into a few scrapes at her boarding school—the usual stuff—sneaking out at night, that kind of thing."

"Where did she go to boarding school?"

He seemed to hesitate, then said, "I doubt you'd know it—it's a private girls' school in the Bellingham area. St. Camille's."

P.J. gave a mental whistle. St. Camille's was pricey. Very pricey. "On scholarship?"

"No. Her father has money. Nothing but the best for his daughter. He's spoiled and indulged her all of her life."

"Sounds like she's her father's only child."

"Yes."

Realizing this was her opportunity to learn more about Alex, P.J. said, "So… your other brothers…they have a different mother than you do?"

He smiled cynically. "Yes."

"Are they younger than you are, too?"

"One of them is."

"One of them? How many brothers do you have?"

At first she thought he wasn't going to answer. But he finally said, "I have three brothers. My father's been married four times. My mother three. As you can see, I have an unorthodox family, and if you don't mind, I really don't want to talk about them anymore. It's not a pleasant subject for me."

He hadn't needed to tell her. P.J. could see her questions had bothered him. Why? she wondered. Was it just because his family didn't fit the all-American mold?

Or was it for a darker reason?

All her old uncertainty about him came rushing back. Was Alex hiding something? And if so, what?

Great, Alex thought. Just great. Now I've roused her suspicions again.

Well, it couldn't be helped. He could hardly refuse to answer her questions. If he had, she'd be even more suspicious than she was now. It was just bad luck that he'd been with P.J. when Julie had called. And he hoped nothing like this would happen again.

Anyway, it wouldn't be long before he could level with P.J. Then there would be no more need to hide anything from her. *In fact, I'll call Cornelia tomorrow. Tell her all about P.J. And if she approves, there will be no more reason to wait at all.*

\* \* \*

"Alex, I would *love* to see you!" Cornelia said. "Come for dinner."

Alex smiled. "What time?"

"How about six-thirty? We'll have cocktails first. I'll call Georgie. Maybe she'll come, too."

After they hung up, Alex walked back through the grounds to the outside entrance of the cafeteria. Spying Rick sitting with a couple of the other guys, he headed for his table. He also saw P.J. sitting and eating with her buddy Anna, but all he did was nod as he walked by. They were being very careful not to let anyone from work know they were seeing each other, and so far he didn't think anyone even suspected. If anyone knew, it would be Anna, and that would only be if P.J. had confided in her.

"I looked for you," Rick said when Alex reached their table, "but you'd already taken off. Where'd you go?"

"I had to make a phone call," Alex said, grabbing a chair and joining the group, which consisted of Rick, Wayne and Jim.

"Uh-oh," Jim said. "Gotta be some chick." He poked Wayne in the arm. "Remember those days, Crowder?"

"Barely," Wayne said. "I've been married too long."

"I had to call my aunt," Alex said.

"Aunt. Sure you did," Jim said.

They laughed and kept kidding him good-naturedly. Alex just let them talk. If they thought he had a girlfriend, great. Then they wouldn't be watching him and P.J.

After lunch was over, Rick and Alex walked back to their quad together.

"Hey, Alex, were you really calling your aunt?" Rick asked.

"Actually, yes. Although she's not really my aunt. She's an old family friend of my father's, but we've always called her our aunt."

"You sure?"

Alex frowned. "What's the problem, Rick?"

Rick hesitated, then blurted out, "I know you've been seein' P.J. and I guess

I just wanted to make sure you aren't stringing her along or anything."

Alex barely managed to keep his mouth from dropping open. "How'd you know about me and P.J.?"

"I got ways. No, seriously, I've seen your truck parked outside her condo a coupla times. And I saw you together at the carnival Saturday."

"Really? I didn't see you."

"I know you didn't. I steered Maria and the kids in the other direction."

"I wouldn't have cared if you'd said hello. In fact, I'd have liked to meet Maria and the girls."

"I know, but I figured maybe P.J. would care. I mean, seein' as how she's your boss and all."

"Is that really a problem?"

"Not for me, it isn't. But I know how P.J. is. She wouldn't want anyone to get the wrong idea. And some of 'em would, Alex. Some might think she was playing favorites, like if you should happen to get a good raise and they should get wind of it."

Alex knew he wouldn't be playing this game of masquerade for much longer. Certainly not long enough to be eligible for a raise.

"Anyway," Rick continued, "I think a lot of P.J. I don't want to see her get hurt."

"I would never hurt P.J."

By now they'd reached the quad and Rick took a stack of orders out of the Fill box by P.J.'s desk.

"Glad to hear it," Rick said, "'cause she's pretty special, you know."

"I do know."

"So is it serious?"

With anyone else, Alex would have been irritated at the questioning, but just as Rick thought a lot of P.J., Alex thought a lot of Rick, and he knew Rick's questions weren't prompted by nosiness but by real concern for P.J.

So Alex answered truthfully. "It is on my part."

Rick nodded thoughtfully.

"I know you said she's not interested in marriage," Alex added. "I hope to change her mind."

A long moment went by before Rick answered. "If anyone can, it'll be you."

P.J. was exhausted and hoped Alex didn't suggest coming over that evening. All she really wanted to do was go home, take a long soak in the tub, maybe give herself a pedicure, have a glass of wine or two, and hunker down in front of the T.V.

Alone.

This was definitely a first in their relationship.

But they'd been together practically nonstop the last few weeks, and a girl needed some time to herself. She especially needed time to think. When P.J. was with Alex, too much of the time she wasn't thinking at all.

But when quitting time rolled around, she didn't even see Alex. And by the time she walked out to the parking lot, his truck was long gone.

Instead of feeling relieved to have her wish granted, she felt annoyed. More than annoyed. Hurt.

Honestly. What was he *doing* to her? She was a mess of contradictions who didn't know what she wanted.

She did know one thing, though.

She should never, *ever,* have started dating him. She'd known from the beginning it was a mistake, and her reaction just now proved it.

If she was disappointed and hurt now, just because he'd left work without saying goodbye or kiss my foot, how was she going to feel when he moved on?

Because he would. Of course he would.

Alex Noble would eventually want to get married. And when he did, he would want someone young and fertile.

And P.J. was neither.

If she had any sense at all, she'd break it off now, while she still had her pride.

"This is so nice," Cornelia said, raising her glass to Alex. "It's been too long since you visited me." She was seated in one of the two rose brocade chairs placed on either side of the fireplace in her living room.

Alex, seated in the other, smiled at her. "It *has* been too long."

Cornelia looked particularly lovely tonight, he thought, in a long black velvet skirt and cream satin blouse. A tall, slender woman, she carried her years lightly, looking a full ten years younger than she was. Her pale hair waved softly around her face, and diamond studs winked in her ears.

Alex had always suspected his father was in love with Cornelia, and he wondered now if she felt the same way.

"So tell me about this young woman you've met," Cornelia said. She sipped at her dry martini.

So Alex told her all about P.J. Everything except the fact she was Peter Prescott Kincaid's daughter. "I think she's perfect for me, and I hope you'll agree, because if you do, so will Harry."

"I see." Her shrewd blue eyes studied

him. "You've fallen in love with her, haven't you?"

Alex blinked. "I—" He stopped. *Was* he in love with P.J.?

Cornelia watched him affectionately.

"Maybe I am," he said slowly. "I don't think I realized it until just this minute."

"Does she have any idea of who you really are?"

"No." Alex chuckled. "And she doesn't know that I know who *she* is."

Cornelia drank a little more of her martini and gave him a curious look.

"She's the daughter of Peter Prescott Kincaid."

Now it was Cornelia's turn to look stunned. "Whatever is she doing working at HuntCom's Distribution Center?"

"Good question. I'm not positive because I haven't revealed what I know about her, but just from our conversations about college, I know she didn't like the corporate world. I also know she shares my world view about excessive wealth and its evils." He finished off his vodka and tonic.

"I hope this doesn't turn out to be a problem."

Alex frowned. "How could it be? I would think Harry would be delighted by her background, since she obviously isn't a gold digger." Once again, he heard the bitterness in his voice.

Cornelia sighed. "Alex, dear, haven't you punished your mother long enough?"

"No offense, but I don't want to discuss my mother."

"No," she murmured. "I'm sure you don't. But surely you realize how your feelings toward her have affected everything in your life."

Alex reached for a cracker and spread it with brie. "Aunt Cornelia..."

"I know, I know. But I can't help trying to effect a reconciliation between you. Lucinda loves you, Alex. And you have no idea how tough it was for her once Harry put pressure on her. But I do."

Alex's jaw hardened. He would never

be rude to Cornelia, but he wished she'd drop the subject. There was nothing she could say that would make him feel any different.

"Back to the subject of your P.J.," Cornelia said. "When I said I hoped there wouldn't be a problem, I meant she might be upset when she finds out who *you* are. Especially if, as you say, she isn't seduced by the thought of money." She raised her eyebrows. "More to the point, though, is the fact you've lied to her."

"For a good reason."

"She might not see it that way."

"Do you really think so?"

"It's very possible. It sounds to me as if she has a great deal of integrity. And pride."

"But she's not exactly playing it straight, either," Alex pointed out.

"Perhaps she hasn't revealed exactly who her father is, but she didn't change her name." Unspoken was *like you did*.

"You know I had no choice."

"I know. It's the one part of your father's

challenge that has bothered me from the beginning. I share his sentiment about young women who—" She broke off as Elizabeth, her long-time housekeeper, appeared in the doorway. "Yes, Elizabeth?"

"Dinner is ready, Mrs. Fairchild."

Cornelia rose gracefully. "Thank you, Elizabeth." She looked at Alex. "Shall we?"

He stood, giving her his arm, and together they walked into the softly lighted dining room. Over succulent rack of lamb, baby peas and tiny new potatoes, they continued to discuss Harry's challenge, then moved on to an update about each of Cornelia's daughters.

"I'm sorry Georgie couldn't make it tonight," Alex said. He grinned. "She doesn't think much of Harry's challenge."

"Oh, I know," Cornelia said with a wry smile. "She gave me an earful about my role in the whole thing. She said she couldn't believe I'd be a party to such shameful blackmail."

Alex laughed. "That's our Georgie. She always says exactly what she thinks."

"And I tried so hard to instill old-fashioned manners in my girls. To no avail, I'm afraid."

"You wouldn't change any of them if you could, and you know it," Alex teased.

Cornelia smiled. "You're right. I wouldn't. I just like to grouse a bit, that's all. It's a mother's prerogative."

Alex almost said, *I wouldn't know,* but thought better of it. The last thing he wanted was to get into another discussion about his own mother.

After a generous slice of Elizabeth's famed butterscotch pie for dessert, Alex leaned back and patted his stomach. "If I ate like this every day, I'd weigh a ton."

"As would I," Cornelia said. "But tonight was a special occasion."

Alex couldn't help feeling guilty that he didn't visit Cornelia more often. He knew she considered him and his brothers almost like her own sons.

Cornelia poured cream into her coffee. "I want you to bring your P.J. to meet me just as soon as you finalize things with her."

"Of course I will."

After they finished their coffee, Alex reluctantly said he'd better be going. "I have a long drive back."

Cornelia walked with him to the front door. When he bent down to kiss her cheek, he thought how much he loved her, and how great it would have been if she'd been his mother instead of Lucinda.

"Don't wait too long to tell P.J. the truth, Alex," was her final piece of advice as he walked out the door into the evening drizzle. "Lies have a way of magnifying the longer they're perpetuated."

Yes, Alex thought, he needed and wanted to tell P.J. the truth. But how could he do that and still fulfill the terms of Harry's conditions?

## *Chapter Eleven*

Alex's cell phone rang Tuesday morning as he was on his way to work. Picking it up, he glanced at the caller ID and saw the number for his office.

"Marti?" he said, knowing it had to be his assistant.

"Oh, Alex, I'm so glad I caught you. We've got a crisis looming. Is there any way you can come into the office today?"

"What kind of crisis?"

"It's Richard Priest."

Alex swore. Richard Priest was an eccentric multi-millionaire who had founded an electronics empire. He was one of the few donors from whom the Hunt Foundation accepted money unquestioningly. This was due to the fact that nothing his companies manufactured or sold conflicted with the purpose or goals of the foundation. But his money came at a price. He'd demanded a seat on the board, and periodically he managed to insult another board member, a donor, and once in a while even a head of state.

"What's he done now?" Alex asked wearily.

"He told Philippa Von Kohler it would be a cold day in hell before KeepKidsWell got another nickel from us."

For a moment, Alex was speechless. KeepKidsWell was the brainchild of Mrs. Von Kohler—widow of the founder of a popular chain of doughnut shops—and she not only ran the charity with an iron hand, she funded fifty percent of its costs herself. KKW, as Alex thought of it, was one his favorite projects. "What the hell brought *that* on?"

"Apparently she gave an interview to Will Crosby and she badmouthed Richard. Said he was an idiot. This is because he disapproves of giving condoms to kids, which she advocates as part of her safe-sex educational program. Anyway, he's called a board meeting for ten o'clock this morning. When I told him I didn't know if I could reach you or not, he said, quote, we don't need Alex as long as we have a majority, unquote."

Alex sighed.

"I think you'd better be here, Alex. You know how he can intimidate some of the board members. I'm afraid he'll get the vote he wants and block that big payment that's supposed to go to KeepKidsWell on the first of the month."

If Alex had had Richard Priest there, he would have throttled the man. "All right, I'll come. It's going to be tight, though. You know what morning traffic is like going into town. Just don't let the meeting start without me."

After disconnecting the call, Alex called P.J. Dammit, anyway. He had to go back to the apartment to call P.J. because he still hadn't done anything about buying a new cell phone. Mentally berating himself, plus crossing his fingers against getting a speeding ticket, he raced back to his complex.

He was relieved when she didn't answer her phone and it went to voice mail. Easier to lie to voice mail than to talk to her in person.

"P.J.," he said, "I'm sorry, but something urgent has come up and I need to take a day of personal leave. If I'm not eligible for leave, just dock my pay. Thanks. I'll call you tonight."

He'd figure out what that "urgent" matter was later. Right now he didn't have time.

It was almost ten o'clock before he reached downtown Seattle—the traffic had been horrendous and the trip that would normally take him ninety minutes had taken two and a half hours. Alex had hoped to make a stop at his apartment there so he could change into a suit, but he didn't have enough time, so his jeans, sweater, and work boots were going to have to suffice.

When he walked into the paneled conference room of the foundation's offices, he had to bite back a smile at the expressions on the faces of the eight board members sitting around the huge cherry-wood table. Greeting them, he saw that Alicia Herman and Jonathan St. Clair were missing. Too bad. They were both realistic members with progressive views on health care and would have been unlikely to be swayed by anything Richard would have to say to the contrary.

Marti smiled at him. "Nice outfit," she murmured as he took his seat at the head of the table. "Want some coffee?"

Alex nodded gratefully. "Thanks."

When she left the room to get his coffee, Richard said, "I didn't know you were going to be here, Alex."

"Wouldn't have missed it," Alex said dryly.

"You're looking well," Lydia Cross, who was a partner in a prestigious Seattle law firm, said. "Have you been traveling?"

Alex kept his answer vague and pretended he hadn't seen the avid curiosity in her eyes.

Once Marti returned and was ready to take the minutes, Alex called the meeting to order. The only agenda item was Richard's request to cut off funding for KeepKidsWell. Alex listened courteously while Richard presented his case and made his recommendation.

Without stopping for questions, Richard said, "I move that—"

"Let's have some discussion before you make a formal motion," Alex said, interrupting before Richard could finish.

"According to Robert's Rules of Order, discussion comes *after* a motion is made," Richard said angrily.

"It can be done either way," Alex contradicted. "And this is the way I'd like to do it."

Richard's jaw clenched, and he glared at Alex.

Alex didn't care. In fact, right now he didn't care if Richard took his money and his weirdness and left the Hunt Foundation for good. Sometimes the price you had to pay to keep things moving smoothly was more than you were willing to pay. And this was one of those times.

"Now," Alex continued, "I agree that Philippa stepped over the line when she called you an idiot in public, Richard, but the fact is, you provoked her. I personally heard you telling Winston over there…" Alex inclined his head toward Winston Legrand, a retired bank president "…that Philippa didn't exhibit good sense and was running KeepKidsWell into the ground. And if you said that to him, I'm sure you've said it to others."

"Too bad if the truth hurts," Richard sputtered.

"Maybe she felt she was expressing the truth, too," Alex said.

There was an audible intake of breath from some of the board members.

"What does *that* mean?" Richard said.

"Just what I said."

"I don't have to sit here and listen to this!" Richard stood so abruptly, he knocked his chair over. "You, young man, think you're God here. You think you can do whatever you want, whenever you want, just because you're Harry's son. Well, let me tell you something. I carry some weight here, too. Let's just take a vote on this and see who's right and who's wrong."

"Sit down, Richard," Alex said calmly.

"I'll stand if I want to." Richard's face had turned a dark, mottled red.

Quietly, yet firmly, Alex said, "As long as I'm chairman of this board, we will conduct our business in a professional, courteous manner. You will either sit down and lower your voice or I will ask you to leave."

A person could have heard a pin drop. No one moved. No one said a word. And although Richard glared at Alex, he reached back, righted his chair, and sat back down. "I demand you let me make my motion."

"Fine," Alex said, "make it."

"I move that the Hunt Foundation stop giving any money to KeepKidsWell and that we permanently strike them from our list of recipients."

"Seconded," said Winston Legrand.

Alex wasn't surprised. He'd figured Winston would vote with Richard. "Any discussion?"

Lydia Cross spoke up. "I think Mrs. Von Kohler exhibited bad judgment by casting doubt about a board member's intelligence, but I don't think her lapse should be held against a charity we all know is doing a remarkable job in helping kids at risk."

"Helping kids have sex is more like it," Winston grumbled.

Richard snorted. "You can say that again."

"The condoms are only given to teens who are already having sex," Lydia pointed out. "And that's to protect them against HIV."

The discussion continued in this vein

for more than twenty minutes, with neither side yielding an inch. Finally Alex said, "If there are no new points to raise, I think it's time for a vote." He didn't know what would happen, but clearly, this discussion was a waste of time.

Alex breathed a sigh of relief when the vote was three in favor of the motion, five against. Alex only voted in the event of a tie, so his vote wasn't needed.

"I won't be a party to this any longer," Richard said. "I'm resigning from this board, and I will no longer lend my financial support to the foundation."

"We're sorry to see you go," Alex said, "but it's your prerogative."

Winston looked as if he was going to say something, but he didn't. Alex almost smiled. Winston liked being on the foundation's board. Since he'd retired, he had too much time on his hands and he no longer felt that people viewed him as important. Being on the board of the Hunt Foundation helped assuage those feelings and gave him opportunities to pretend he was still a mover and shaker.

After everyone had gone home, Marti said, "God, I miss you, Alex. When are you going to be done with whatever it is you're doing?"

"Soon, I hope." Alex looked at his watch. It was almost noon. It was too late to worry about going into work at the distribution center today. Besides, he wasn't sure he wanted to see P.J. until he had a good story for her. "What else do I need to catch up on here? I can give you a few more hours."

Marti smiled. "Well, since you asked…"

"P.J., you're not going to believe this!" Anna's voice fairly quivered with excitement.

P.J. wasn't in the mood for gossip. She'd been working for hours, and she couldn't make her inventory and her orders balance. No matter how many times she added her columns, she had more equipment in several categories than she was supposed to have. And in two other categories, she had less than she should. "What?" she said impatiently.

"I don't want to tell you over the phone. Come to the mail room and I'll show you."

"Anna, I'm up to my eyeballs in—"

"P.J., I'm telling you, you want to see this." She lowered her voice. "It's about Alex."

"Alex? You mean Alex who works here?"

"What other Alex is there?" Anna said dryly. "Now get your butt over here. Hurry. You're going to die when you see this."

Five minutes later, P.J. entered the busy mailing center and headed straight for Anna's office, which was in the far corner. Anna sat behind her desk and when she spied P.J., she beckoned her in.

"Close the door," she said. Her dark eyes sparkled with excitement.

"This had better be good," P.J. said.

"C'mere." Anna had an open magazine on her desk.

P.J. walked around to stand next to

Anna. The magazine was one of those celebrity rags Anna was so fond of. P.J. started to say something derogatory when she saw what Anna was pointing to. It was a photo in a section called VIPs. P.J. looked closer, then snatched up the magazine. She stared at the photo. It showed a beautiful, dark-haired young girl in a yellow dress seated across from a slightly older man who was a dead ringer for Alex. They were obviously in a restaurant, leaning toward each other intimately and talking.

P.J. swallowed. The caption under the photo read:

Julie Fitzpatrick, who is usually part of the Seattle club scene, shown on a recent Sunday enjoying a quiet brunch with her half-brother, Alex Hunt, son of Harrison Hunt, billionaire founder of HuntCom.

Alex *Hunt!*
P.J.'s heart pounded in her ears. She

kept staring at the photo. She couldn't believe it. Alex. Her Alex was really Alex Hunt.

"P.J.?"

P.J. blinked. She'd almost forgotten Anna was there.

"Can you *believe* it?" Anna said. "You were right all the time. You thought he didn't belong here. What do you think he's doing here, anyway?"

"Can I have this magazine?" P.J. said. "Or at least this page?"

Anna frowned. "Um…sure."

P.J.'s hands trembled as she tore the page from the magazine. She was so angry and so upset, she wasn't sure she could talk to Anna. Thank God she'd never told Anna that she was seeing Alex. She almost had, one day, but had changed her mind at the last minute. It had been the only rational decision she'd ever made concerning Alex.

*Oh, God. Hunt. He's a Hunt. Harrison Hunt's son. No wonder he didn't want to talk about his family. He's been lying to me the whole time I've known him. Everything about him is a lie. Everything he's said. Everything he's done.*

She couldn't look at Anna, but she knew she had to say something. "Don't tell anyone about this, okay? Let me deal with it first."

"Okay. What are you going to do?"

"I don't know. I have to think about it."

Anna nodded. "I didn't think you'd be so upset."

P.J. knew she needed to get a grip. Anna was suspicious now, and that's the last thing P.J. wanted. "I just don't like being lied to. He was probably sent here to spy on us."

"You think?"

"Why else?"

"But we do a great job here. That just doesn't make sense."

"Look," P.J. said, "I've got to get back to my desk. Remember. Don't say anything about this."

"I won't."

P.J. knew Anna was probably frowning as she watched P.J. leave and head back to the floor. But right then, P.J. didn't care what Anna thought. All *she* could think about was what a fool she'd been. Oh, God, she thought, remembering the way she'd offered absolutely no resistance to Alex. She'd been like putty in his hands. And all the time, he'd just been toying with her. Amusing himself while putting in his time as some kind of spy for his father.

She thought about how concerned she'd been when she got his message this morning. How she'd even considered covering for him because he was right; he hadn't worked there long enough to have a personal day. Oh! How could she have been so stupid?

And to think she'd even been going to tell him about her medical problems, feeling it was unfair to keep seeing him without letting him know she was damaged goods. Tears stung her eyes, and that made her madder still. She *never* cried! Crying was weak, and she wasn't weak.

By the time she reached her desk, she had managed to get herself under some kind of control, because she needed to think. She was suddenly very glad Alex wasn't there today, because when she confronted him, she wanted to be calm and prepared.

"P.J."

She jumped. Chick, her assistant, stood there frowning down at her. "Yes, Chick?"

"Everything okay?"

"Why wouldn't it be?" she snapped.

"I don't know. I just thought—"

She almost said, *Don't think*. In the nick of time, she stopped herself and said instead, "I'm fine. Did you need something?"

He shook his head and backed away. "No, no. I just wanted to see—" This time he broke off. "Never mind. I'm going back to work."

"Good. See if you can have the weekly report on my desk by…" She made a show of looking at her watch. "Two o'clock."

Chick saluted. "Your wish is my command."

P.J. was ashamed of herself. She hadn't been very nice to Chick, and aside from Rick, he was her most valuable employee. This, too, could be laid at Alex Noble/Hunt's door, she thought bitterly.

For the rest of the afternoon, she didn't even try to work. She knew it would be a lost cause. Instead, she looked up everything she could find about Alex Hunt on the Internet. The more she learned, the more confused she became. He was nothing like what she would have imagined a son of Harrison Hunt to be. He wasn't a playboy. He didn't do the party circuit. He didn't constantly have some gorgeous model or actress on his arm. And he didn't throw his money around. According to a profile the Seattle paper had done on him several years ago, Alex Hunt lived quietly and worked hard. He'd headed the Hunt Foundation for ten years, and according to all reports, it was his passion.

In an article about one of the charities supported by the Hunt Foundation, there was the text of a speech he'd given at the charity's annual fund-raiser. P.J. found herself nodding as she read what he'd said. She agreed with every word.

At the end of the day, she didn't know what to think. Everything she'd learned about Alex indicated he held the same beliefs she held. That he was a man she could admire and respect.

But if that was true, why was he working at the distribution center? Why had he lied?

None of it made sense.

And none of it changed the fact that P.J. felt like the biggest fool who had ever lived.

While Alex was in Seattle, he had decided to take care of some things. He decided to stay in the city overnight and do the things he hadn't been able to do from Jansen, like visit his bank, touch base with a couple of his pet charities, and take Georgie to dinner.

He'd put off calling P.J. but once he was back in his Seattle apartment, he knew he couldn't stall any longer. So at ten o'clock, he placed the call.

The phone at the other end rang four times. Then it revolved to voice mail. "This is P.J.," the message began. "Can't take your call right now. At the tone, leave a message."

Alex frowned. Where was she? he wondered. "Hey, P.J., it's me, Alex. I'm on my way back to Jansen, but I probably won't get there until late. I'll see you in the morning."

Since he would have to leave the city by five-thirty to insure getting to the distribution center on time tomorrow, Alex decided to call it a night.

Thirty minutes later, he was sound asleep.

P.J. stared at the phone.

She didn't pick up.

She had no desire to talk to Alex tonight. Not on the phone. She wanted to face him when he lied to her. She wanted to see his face when she confronted him with what she knew about him.

Right now, that was about the only satisfaction she was likely to have in this whole sorry affair.

If only it didn't hurt so much.

If only she could just laugh this off.

After all, as Courtney had pointed out, *she* wasn't who she was pretending to be, either.

But the situations were entirely different. She had never lied to Alex. Any question he'd ever asked her, she had answered truthfully, whereas he'd lied to her from the get-go.

Well, never again.

Never, never, never again.

This time, P.J. had learned her lesson. She'd thought Alex was different. She'd even begun to imagine the possibility of a future with him. Even begun to think that maybe her medical problems wouldn't matter to him. Even begun to admit to herself that she was falling in love with him and had harbored a secret hope that he felt the same way.

Tears ran down her face as the truth sank in.

Alex didn't love her.

And now he never would.

## *Chapter Twelve*

P.J. arrived at the distribution center before seven. She knew she looked terrible, with dark circles under her eyes that no amount of makeup could disguise. She'd had a bad night, had tossed and turned and slept fitfully. And what little sleep she'd been able to manage had been filled with dark dreams where she was lost in some kind of horrible maze, and no matter what she did or which way she turned, she couldn't find her way out.

You didn't have to be a psychiatrist or analyst to know the significance of *that* dream, she thought wryly.

"You're here early."

P.J. managed a smile for Terri Wayland, the night supervisor on the floor. "Yeah, I've got a few things hanging fire. Thought I'd get an early start."

"Anything I can help with?"

"Thanks, no. But I appreciate the offer."

"Okay. Just holler if you need me." Terri waved and walked away.

P.J. headed for the kitchen, got herself a cup of coffee, then walked across to her office. After closing the door firmly, she booted her computer. Once it was finished loading programs, she opened Word and began composing a letter.

At eight o'clock, as the day shift began coming in, she opened her office door and strode out onto the floor. A glance at the time cards showed that Alex had already clocked in. She was just about to look for him when she saw him walking toward her. As usual, he was dressed in jeans, work boots, and today—a chilly, late October day—a red plaid flannel shirt with a black T-shirt underneath. Unfortunately for her, he looked even more handsome and sexy than usual. He held a mug of coffee.

"'Morning," he said, giving her one of his dimpled smiles. "I wanted to apologize for yester—"

"Let's go into my office," she said, interrupting him. She didn't return his smile.

His smile slowly faded. She could see he was startled by her abrupt tone. Good. He obviously had no idea she was on to him. Not waiting to see if he was following her, she turned and marched off.

By the time she reached her office, her hard-won calm had disappeared and she was seething. God, he must think she was stupid. *Well, he's right, isn't he?* Once they were both inside the office, she shut the door and gave him a hard-eyed stare.

"P.J., what's wrong? I know I shouldn't have taken off without asking you first, but it couldn't be—"

Once more she interrupted him. "I'll tell you what's wrong, Alex. *This* is what's wrong." She grabbed the page she'd torn from the magazine, which was sitting on the edge of her desk, and thrust it at him.

He frowned. "What's this?"

"Just read it." She jabbed her finger at the offending photo. "That."

Her chest felt too tight and her head pounded from a killer headache that no amount of Advil had been able to banish. He finished reading and lowered the page. His dark eyes, eyes that she loved—*had* loved, she corrected—met her gaze. Although she was trembling inside, she told herself she could do this. *This isn't the first time you've had to face something painful. Grit your teeth. Don't let him see how much you're hurting.*

"P.J.," he said softly. "I can explain."

"Really?" she scoffed.

"It…I know it looks bad, but there's a reason for—"

"For pretending to be someone you're not? For lying to me?"

"The only thing I lied about is my name…and my reason for being here. Everything else was the truth."

"Why the hell *are* you here, Alex? Was I right in the beginning? Were you sent here to spy on us?"

"No." He walked over and put his coffee on the desk. "Absolutely not. My reasons for being here are personal. They have nothing to do with the business or the job you're doing here or anything remotely like that."

She glared at him. How could he continue to lie to her? And with such sincerity, too? If she didn't know better, she'd absolutely believe him. Fury and heartbreak warred within as she fought to maintain control of emotions that threatened to erupt. "I can't believe you are *still* lying to me. What possible personal reason could you have for leaving the Hunt Foundation, which is supposedly so important to you? Oh, yes," she added, seeing the surprise on his face. "I read about you. I read all about you."

"I…" He seemed to be struggling with himself. Finally, with a heavy sigh, he said, "Look, P.J., can we sit down? I'll explain everything."

P.J. wanted to say no. She wanted to tell him to get out of her office. But he was Alex Hunt, wasn't he? He was the son of the owner of HuntCom and she was just an employee. She actually worked for *him*, not the other way around. "Fine," she said. She walked behind her desk and sat in her swivel chair.

Alex sat across from her.

Why did he have to look so damned gorgeous? Obviously, *he'd* had a great night's sleep. She certainly didn't see any bags under *his* eyes. "Well?" she said coldly. "I'm waiting."

"The reason I'm here is because of my father."

"I figured that."

"It's not what you think. Do you know much about my father? His personal life, that is?"

P.J. shrugged.

Seeing she wasn't going to help him out, he said, "He was married four times. None of his marriages lasted longer than two years. Each marriage produced a son. When I told you I was one of four brothers, that's the truth. Neither I nor my brothers have ever been married." He grimaced. "We didn't have a great example of marriage."

P.J. wished she had a fresh cup of coffee. Anything to occupy her hands. Anything to wrest her gaze from his.

"Last spring my father had a heart attack. It was a pretty serious one, and it scared him."

P.J. nodded. She remembered. At the time, Steve Mallery had been concerned about what would happen if Harrison Hunt died.

"Afterwards," Alex continued, "he seemed different. More reflective. I guess he finally realized he wasn't indestructible and wouldn't live forever." Alex smiled crookedly. "Anyway, he called a meeting of the four of us—me and my brothers—

in July, and told us he was tired of waiting for us to get married and give him grand-children. He said, quote, left to our devices, he never would have any, un-quote. He said a few other things…then he gave us an ultimatum. Within a year, he wanted each of us married, and by the end of that time, he also wanted our wives to be pregnant or already to have given birth."

P.J. wasn't sure she'd heard him cor-rectly. "You're kidding, right?"

"No, unfortunately, I'm not. That wasn't the end of the ultimatum, either. The women we married couldn't be gold diggers. My father isn't big on gold diggers," Alex added sarcastically, "because he married enough of them himself. To accomplish this, he said we couldn't tell our prospective brides who we were. That was the only way we could be sure they were marrying us for our-selves and not for his money."

As what Alex told her sank in, P.J. stared at him, appalled. "And this is why you *lied* to me? Because of some kind of stupid agreement you made with your father? You're here at HuntCom looking for a *bride?*"

"I'm sorry, P.J. I didn't want to lie to you. But I had no choice. If I'd told you who I really was, I would have been letting my brothers down. Hell, I'm letting them down *now*. See, that's the way Harry got us to agree to his scheme. He threatened to sell the entire corporation, everything that makes up HuntCom, including the foundation, which is my passion, and the special projects and places that are important to my brothers."

P.J. couldn't believe what she was hearing. This whole situation had been bad enough when she'd thought Alex was a corporate spy. *That*, at least, she could understand. She didn't have to like it, but she could understand it. "So this is about money."

"It's not about money."

"Oh, of course it is. You can dress it up any way you like but at the root of everything is money. Your father certainly understands that."

"I don't care about the money. I do care about the foundation and the work we're doing, but I would even have given that up if I'd had to. But my father put one other condition on his proposal to us—we all had to agree. If even one of us didn't, all of us would lose out. I couldn't do that to my brothers."

"So you went along with his nutty scheme that's like something out of the Dark Ages. You came here under false pretenses and you lied to me and everyone else. Tell me, Alex, just when *did* you plan to tell me the truth? Or didn't I figure into your plans at all? Was I just some kind of side diversion while you were looking for the perfect, gullible candidate to be Mrs. Alex Hunt?" She was trying not to think about the baby Alex had mentioned. The baby Harrison Hunt had ordered. The baby P.J. could never give him.

He stared at her. "How can you say that? You must know it's not true. I was attracted to you from the moment I met you." He heaved a sigh. "Look, this isn't the way I'd have chosen to say this. I'd rather be doing it over wine and candlelight. The truth is, I love you, P.J. I'd want you to be my wife even if my father'd had nothing to do with my meeting you."

"You expect me to *believe* that? How can I ever believe another word you say? By your own admission, you *have* to go along with your father's demands, so you'd say anything to keep from upsetting your little applecart."

"I've already upset it. You know who I am, so I've broken my father's rules."

P.J. gripped her hands below the desk to keep them from shaking. She wanted, more than anything, to believe him, but how could she? And what if she *did* believe him? What good would it do her? She couldn't give him a child. When he found out about that, he would no longer want her, anyway.

"You know, you haven't exactly been playing it straight either, P.J., or should I say…Paige."

She wasn't even surprised he knew about her family. "Don't try to make this about me, Alex. I repudiated my family's money. But *you!* You did what you did *for* the money. And nothing you can say will ever change my mind about that." Then she reached for the letter she'd typed that morning and handed it to him.

"What is this?" he said.

"It's my letter of resignation."

"Don't be ridiculous." Without even looking at it, he ripped the letter in two, then in four, then in eight, throwing the pieces in the wastebasket. "If you want to quit, go talk to Steve Mallery. He's your boss, not me. But I'll save you the trouble. I'll leave instead. In fact, I'll go right now. Unless you want two weeks notice?"

She swallowed. She wanted to say, *Please don't go.* But she didn't say anything.

Ten seconds later, he walked out the door. He didn't look back.

"Hey, Alex, what's going on?"

Alex was angry and frustrated, and the

last thing he wanted to do was talk to anyone, but he could hardly ignore Rick. "Look, I can't talk right now. But if you want, we can meet for a beer after work."

"*Meet* for a beer? Where're you going?"

"I'll explain later, okay? Right now, I have to get out of here." Alex gestured toward P.J.'s office. "But if you can't wait till tonight, you could always go ask P.J. what's going on. She's got all the answers."

"Oh, Alex," Cornelia said. "I was afraid of this."

"Yeah," he said glumly. "I guess I should have been worried, but somehow I thought everything would work out."

"Did you tell her you love her?"

"Yes, but I handled it badly. She doesn't believe me."

Cornelia sighed. "Shall I try to talk to her?"

He shook his head. "This is something I have to do. First I'm going to let her cool off. Then I'll try talking to her again." He looked up, and the sympathetic look on his aunt's face was nearly his undoing. "I don't want to lose her, Aunt Cornelia. Even if it means losing the foundation and J.T., Justin and Gray losing the ranch and the island and the company."

"She's that important to you?"

"Yes."

"Then do whatever it takes to get her back, Alex. Don't let anything, especially not pride, stand in your way. Because love like that doesn't come along very often. And it rarely comes twice."

P.J. didn't last the day. At two o'clock, she could no longer keep up the pretense that all was normal. She told Chick she wasn't feeling well and was going home.

"You're going *home?*" he said in disbelief.

"Yes." She knew what he was thinking. P.J. never took a sick day. In fact, in the nearly eight years she'd been with the company, she could count on one hand the amount of days she'd missed, and two of them were when she was called for jury duty.

She barely made it to her car before she burst into tears. She, Paige Jeffers Kincaid, tough girl, someone who never cried, bawled her eyes out.

She was still crying when she arrived at her condo.

She cried off and on all evening. She'd stop, decide to quit feeling sorry for herself, tell herself she wasn't the first woman to be taken in by brown eyes and dimples, then she'd start crying again.

The phone rang once. She looked at it, then jumped up to see who it was.

*Alex.*

She put the phone back in its base. She didn't want to talk to him. What was there left to say?

*Maybe he does love you. Maybe it wouldn't matter to him that you can't have a baby. Maybe he'd want to marry you, anyway.*

Oh, sure. And give up his foundation? Give up all that money? Give up the chance to have dozens of little Alex Hunts? Yeah, and pigs can now fly.

*You could test him.*

But if she did, and if he failed the test, she knew she would be so devastated, she might not be able to pretend otherwise. At least this way, she still did have her pride.

*And not much else.*

On and on her thoughts raged. But the outcome was always the same. Alex was history.

*Get over it! It's not the end of the world. It's not the death of a child. It's just the end of a love affair you always knew was going to end anyway.*

And then the tears started again.

Finally, at midnight, she fell into an exhausted sleep.

Alex's night wasn't much better than P.J.'s. He met Rick for a beer after work and told him the whole sorry tale. Rick just kept shaking his head.

"Geez, Alex. You sure have made a

mess of things," he said when Alex finally wound down.

"Tell me about it."

"Are you *really* old Harry's son?"

"Afraid so," Alex said dejectedly.

"You know, if this wasn't so damned serious, and if it didn't involve P.J., who I think the world of, it would be funny."

"Really? You think it's funny?" Alex said. He finished off his beer and ordered another.

"Think about it. You're a millionaire pretending to be an ordinary Joe, and P.J., also no slouch in the money department, is pretending to be an ordinary Jane. I mean, it's like a comedy. It could be a movie."

Alex smiled. Rick had a point. "It's a comedy of errors."

"Look," Rick said, finishing off his own beer, "I know P.J. She's got a temper and she's stubborn. She would also hate thinking she'd been made to look like a fool. But she's also smart and I think she probably really cares for you, so if you keep after her, she'll probably come around."

"You think?"

"Worth a try. I mean, what have you got to lose?"

Alex thought about what Cornelia had said and what Rick had said and knew they were both right. He decided not to wait until morning, when he'd planned to try to talk to P.J. again. Instead, he called her as soon as he got to his apartment, but there was no answer. When her voice mail kicked in, he decided not to leave a message. He would call her tomorrow.

Better yet, he would go to see her tomorrow. He would sit in front of her condo until she came home and she wouldn't be able to avoid him. She would have to listen to him.

And this time, he would not take no for an answer.

## Chapter Thirteen

Over the next two weeks, Alex tried everything. He called P.J. He cornered her at her condo. He sent e-mails. He sent flowers. He sent a singing telegram. He wrote her a long letter.

Nothing worked.

She kept saying no.

The week before Thanksgiving, he decided to play his trump card. He drove to Bellevue, went into Tiffany's, and bought the prettiest rose-cut diamond ring they had. He knew better than to get something ostentatious, so he settled for a one-carat stone set in platinum. Understated and elegant.

When he got back to Jansen, he called her and asked if he could come and see her that night for "one last time."

"Alex, it's over. Why can't you just accept that?"

"Thing is, I'm leaving Jansen. I just wanted to say goodbye. And I have something for you that I wanted to give you before I go," he added quickly, before she could point out that they could just as easily say goodbye by phone.

She sighed. "Okay. You can come. But make it early because I'm going out at seven-thirty."

"I'll be there by six."

Promptly at six, Alex rang her doorbell. The Tiffany's box was safely secured in the zippered pocket of his leather jacket. His heart turned over when she opened the door. She looked tired.

More than tired. Sad.

And he knew he was the cause of that sadness. He'd hurt her and now she'd erected a barrier around her heart, and so far, he hadn't been able to get past it. It was the first time in his adult life he hadn't been able to accomplish a goal he'd set for himself, and Alex didn't like the feeling. More than that, he hated that he was the reason for the wounded expression in her eyes.

"Come on in," she said.

She invited him to sit on the sofa in her living room, but he said he'd rather stand. "I'm not going to keep you long."

There was an awkward silence for a few seconds. Then they both spoke at once.

"So you're leaving," she said.

"I've really missed you," he said.

She didn't smile. "What is it you want, Alex?"

"You know what I want."

"Tonight, I meant."

"Tonight and every night," he said, looking into her eyes.

She swallowed and backed up, even though he hadn't come any closer.

Deciding it was make-or-break time, Alex unzipped the pocket containing the Tiffany's box, removed it and held it out.

"Wh-what is that?" she whispered, backing up even more.

This time, he stepped forward until she had nowhere else to go. Now only a foot separated them and he could smell the combination of the light fragrance she wore and the lemony shampoo she used on her hair.

"P.J., I love you. I never thought I could fall in love like this. More than anything, I want us to be together." He reached for her hand and put the box into it. "Please say you'll marry me. But if you're determined not to marry, then I'll be content for us to just live together. And if that doesn't prove to you that I don't care about my father's money, then I guess nothing ever will."

She stared at the box. And then, shocking him, her eyes filled with tears. She shook her head and held her hand out. "I—I can't take this, Alex. I can't marry you. Please stop asking me. Because the answer is always going to be the same."

"P.J...." He didn't take the box.

"I want you to go now." She pushed the box back into his pocket.

"This doesn't make sen—"

"Goodbye, Alex." She'd brushed the tears away.

He didn't know what else to say. He could see she wasn't going to be swayed. There was something here he didn't understand, something she wasn't telling him, but what it could be, he couldn't imagine.

She walked to the door and opened it.

*Okay,* he thought, *I'll go. But this isn't the end of this. Hunts don't quit. They just regroup for another time.*

He walked to the door, but before going out, he bent down and kissed her. Although she held herself stiffly, he felt her body's reaction.

*She loves me. She can deny it as many times as she wants, but I know she loves me.*

"Take care of yourself," he said softly.

"You, too."

The door shut firmly behind him.

P.J. was so sick of herself. So sick of crying. So sick of being the kind of woman she had always despised. Why? Why had she let Alex get under her skin this way?

*Please, God,* she prayed. *Please help me get over him. Because I can't live this way. And I don't know what to do to change things.*

Alex took care of everything that needed taking care of in Jansen. He paid his landlord the necessary amount to get out of his lease. He closed his Jansen bank account, settled with the utility companies and cancelled the phone and cable service.

He called Goodwill and gave them all his furniture and most of his distribution-center work clothes. He donated the television set to the local women's shelter. Then he packed up the few belongings he was keeping, tossed the bags in the bed of his truck, and drove back to Seattle.

"Hey, Rick, what's going on with P.J.? Jenny said she's taken a leave of absence." Jenny was the switchboard operator at the distribution center.

"Hi, Alex. Yeah, she left right before Thanksgiving and she won't be back till January second."

"Where'd she go?"

"I don't know. She just said she needed a vacation. I, uh, kind of figured it might have something to do with you."

"Damn," Alex muttered. "Do you think she's staying with her family?" Alex had tried her at home and been told by a recording that her number had been changed and the new number was unlisted. And when he'd tried her cell phone, he got a message saying that number was no longer in service. It was obvious she was deliberately cutting him out of her life.

"Like I said, she didn't say what her plans were."

"If you hear from her, would you let me know?"

Rick hesitated. "Thing is, Alex, I really don't want to be in the middle of this. P.J.'s been my friend a long time, and—"

"I understand," Alex said wearily. "You're right. I shouldn't have put you on the spot like that."

They talked awhile more, Alex asking about Maria and the kids, Rick asking about Alex's job at the foundation, then they promised they'd get together before too long, and hung up.

Alex sat at his desk and thought a few minutes. Then he made a couple of phone calls and on the third try got what he wanted—the private number of the Kincaid family home. Two minutes later, he was listening to it ring.

"Kincaid residence," said a soft female voice.

"This is Alex Hunt. May I speak with Paige, please?"

"Miss Paige?"

"Yes."

"I'm sorry, sir, but Miss Paige isn't here."

"When do you expect her back?"

"No, you misunderstood. Miss Paige doesn't live here."

"I know," Alex said, "but I understood that she was staying there for the holidays."

"No, sir, I'm sorry, she's not."

"You wouldn't happen to have a number where I could reach her?"

"I'm sorry, Mr. Hunt. I cannot give out that kind of information. If you want to leave a message, I'll be happy to give it to her if she should call here."

Alex heaved a frustrated sigh after thanking the housekeeper or whoever it was who had answered the phone and disconnected the call. He wondered if P.J.'s e-mail address was still the same. He was sure her work e-mail was unchanged, but he didn't want to send her a message that way. No telling who might read her e-mail while she was gone. And e-mail was totally unsatisfactory, anyway.

He was back to square one.

With no idea how to advance.


P.J. loved Italy. It suited her perfectly. The weather, the people, the food, the wine, the attitude. She especially loved that nothing there reminded her of Alex. It had been worth borrowing against her 401(k) plan to come.

She spent a week in Venice, then moved on to Florence, then to the hills of Tuscany. In Tuscany, she rented a small villa. Even now, in December, the sun shone, the flowers bloomed and the sky was filled with a golden light she'd never seen anywhere else. It was glorious. If she'd been a painter, she'd have tried to capture the beauty of the place. If she'd been a musician, she'd have composed something glorious there, she was sure of it.

She was neither; all she could do was be thankful for the chance to experience the country's wonder.

She healed in Italy. Yes, she still felt melancholy at times, but the constant pain subsided and she grew—if not happy— then content.

But Italy wasn't reality.

And sooner or later, everyone had to face reality. So on her birthday—three days before Christmas—she packed up her things, locked the villa, drove her rental car back to Florence, and flew home.

It took Alex some time, but with persistent digging, he obtained the home phone number of P.J.'s sister Courtney.

"Hello, Alex," she said after he'd introduced himself. "I've heard a lot about you."

He quickly explained what he wanted.

"Where do you live?" she asked.

Taken aback, he said, "I have an apartment in downtown Seattle. Why?"

"Would you like to meet me for lunch tomorrow? I think it's better if we talk in person." She named a small restaurant that was fairly close to his office.

The next day, Alex arrived at the restaurant at twelve-forty-five. He'd made the reservation for one o'clock and had wanted to be early. Courtney was shown to the table a few minutes after one. Although her coloring was very different from P.J.'s, he could see the family resemblance, especially in the shape of her eyes and her smile.

She was very attractive and very pregnant, which—in his eyes—only added to her appeal.

After she was seated and they'd placed their orders, she said, "Paige would kill me if she knew I was here."

He nodded. Knowing P.J., he was sure Courtney was right. "Why *are* you here?"

"Because I know Paige loves you, and I want her to be happy."

"And I love *her*. But it doesn't seem to be doing me any good. Where *is* she, anyway?"

"Actually, she should be home today. Not in Jansen, though. She's going to spend the holidays with our parents."

"Where was she?"

"She went to Italy."

"What can I do to convince her to marry me?"

Courtney eyed him thoughtfully. "Tell me something, Alex. Does your wanting to marry her have anything to do with that crazy scheme of your father's?"

"No."

"You're sure?"

"Positive."

Still she studied him, as if trying to make up her mind about him. "I want to tell you something, but I'll be betraying a confidence. Very few people know about this, and that's how Paige wanted to keep it."

Alarm bells went off in Alex's mind. Was P.J. sick? Did she have some kind of terrible disease? Is that what was behind her refusal to marry him? He was almost afraid to hear what Courtney had to say.

Just then their waiter came with their food, and they stopped talking until he was gone again.

"Please tell me," Alex said. He ignored his lunch.

Courtney sighed heavily. "Six years ago, Paige had to have one of her ovaries removed. She'd been having a lot of pain, and tests revealed that her right ovary was badly infected. They couldn't save it. The following year she developed endometriosis. Do you know anything about that?"

"No, I don't."

"I'm not going to try to explain it. If you want to know more about it, you can research it on the Internet. However, most women who get it have problems getting pregnant. Because Paige only has one ovary and because the endometriosis affected it, there's very little chance she can ever get pregnant. That's why she's been saying no to you, Alex. She knows she can never give you children."

Alex was stunned. At first, the knowledge dismayed him, but it wasn't long before he realized it made no difference to him. He still loved P.J. and he still wanted to marry her. Hell, they could adopt kids. Half a dozen of them, if she wanted.

Courtney smiled. "You don't care," she said softly.

Alex smiled back. "No, I don't."

She picked up her fork to begin eating her salad. "Now I know why P.J. loves you. Of course, the fact that you're gorgeous doesn't hurt."

Alex laughed, the first real laugh he'd had in weeks. Then he, too, began to eat his lunch.

P.J. would be glad when the day was over. She'd always loved Christmas, but this Christmas had been hard for her. Her composure had threatened to crack several times, especially during the family's traditional carol-singing around the piano, and the effort to keep a smile on her face had exhausted her.

If only …

But all the if onlys in the world wouldn't change a thing. Alex was no longer part of her life. The sooner she was able to accept that gracefully, the better off she'd be.

"So do you have any plans for tomorrow?" Courtney said, coming over to where P.J. stood.

P.J. shrugged. "I thought I might hit the sales."

"You? Shopping? Has hell frozen over?"

P.J. couldn't help laughing. "I need some new workout clothes and I know the shopping is better here than it is in Jansen."

"How about if I come with you?"

"You don't really want to do that, do you?"

"Sure. It'll be fun. We can have lunch out, then shop till we drop. Well, until I drop, anyway."

"Well…" P.J. didn't really want to make a day of it. Yet what else did she have to do?

"I'll come by about eleven-thirty," Courtney said. "Brad's on vacation. He can stay home with the kids." She grinned. "Do him good."

Later, as P.J. prepared for bed, she thought about how much she loved Courtney. And all her family. Her mother got under her skin sometimes, but she still loved her. Thinking about all the things she'd never have—a husband, children, grandchildren—she could feel herself getting weepy again. This made her mad. *Stop that. Moping around and feeling sorry for yourself does no one any good, especially not you. Suck it up. Act like an adult.*

But it was so hard.

Much harder than she would ever have believed.

P.J. decided to wear something dressier than her standard pants and casual blouse. So she unearthed a soft forest-green wool skirt and paired it with an ivory cashmere sweater and high-heeled boots. Now she wouldn't embarrass Courtney, who, even six months pregnant, always looked stylish.

P.J.'s parents had left the house about nine to attend a brunch and bridge party given by some friends, so P.J. and the housekeeper were the only ones home. P.J. went downstairs to wait for Courtney and settled herself in the living room where she could look at the tree—a giant Douglas fir trimmed in gold and white.

*If I ever have a tree, it'll be traditional, with all colors of balls and tinsel and multicolored lights. A real family-type tree.*

Oh, God, she was pathetic. She couldn't seem to make her mind go in a different direction. Every single thought she'd had since coming home from Italy had somehow been tied to husbands, kids, families.

*I wish I could have stayed there forever.*

Restless, she got up and stood at the big bay window. It was a pretty day outside—cold but sunny. She was glad now that Courtney had suggested their day together. As she watched, a silver SUV turned into the drive and slowly came up the hill toward the house.

P.J. frowned. Who was coming? She didn't recognize the truck.

A moment later, the SUV entered the circle in front of the house and came to a stop. And a moment after that, the driver's-side door opened and...*oh, my God*...it was Alex! Sudden panic filled her. And yet, as he got out of the SUV and walked to the door, she stood frozen at the window. She couldn't take her eyes off him. Dressed in dark gray slacks and a matching sweater worn under a black suede jacket, he looked sophisticated and handsome and...wonderful.

Heart pounding, P.J. finally moved, went into the front hallway and, taking a deep breath, opened the door. *Please, God, let me be strong.* For long seconds, they simply looked at each other.

Then Alex smiled. "Aren't you going to invite me in?"

P.J. licked her lips. She was fiercely glad she had taken pains with her appearance today. "What are you doing here, Alex?"

"I came because I have something to tell you, and afterwards—after we talk—

I'm hoping you'll let me take you to lunch."

"I already have a lunch date."

"Courtney's not coming," he said softly.

P.J. tried not to let the shock she felt show on her face. "You've talked to Courtney?"

"Are you going to make me stand out here all day?" he countered.

Mind whirling with the implications of what he'd revealed, P.J. stepped back and gestured him in. "Let's go into the living room." She led the way, all the while telling herself not to lose her cool. *But when I get my hands on Courtney, I'll kill her.*

She deliberately chose one of the Queen Anne chairs on either side of the fireplace. Alex, though, didn't sit. Instead, absolutely shocking her, he dropped down on one knee in front of her.

"P.J.," he said, "I'm not going to waste time. We've already wasted enough time. I love you more than I thought I could ever love anyone, and I want you to be my wife. Courtney told me about your fertility problem and it doesn't make one iota of difference to me. I still want to marry you, and if we decide we want children, we'll adopt them. Now I'm not moving and I'm not leaving until you say yes."

And then he reached into his jacket pocket and pulled out a velvet box.

She looked into his eyes and saw the truth of what he'd said. And suddenly, the way she had too many times to count over the past week, she burst into tears.

Without a word, Alex stood and, taking P.J.'s hand, helped her to her feet. Then, setting the Tiffany's box on the table beside her, he put his arms around her and kissed her. And as P.J. responded, twining her arms around him and giving herself up to the kiss, she knew this was where she belonged, right here, with Alex, who really did love her after all.

Eventually P.J. repaired her makeup and Alex took her to lunch. He couldn't stop smiling, and it seemed, neither could she. In fact, they spent a lot of time just looking at each other and smiling like fools.

But after lunch, Alex knew it was time to get serious. "How would you feel about eloping?" he said.

"Eloping?"

"Yes."

"When?"

"Today."

"Today?"

He grinned. "Are you going to repeat everything I say?"

She laughed sheepishly. "I'm sorry."

God, she was adorable. He loved everything about her. Her wild red hair. Those incredible blue eyes. Her pale redhead skin with the smattering of freckles on her breastbone. Her strong body. Her stronger mind and convictions. Her honesty and courage. She was perfect.

"Here's what I thought we could do. Fly to Vegas, get married tonight or tomorrow, depending on when we get the license, spend two nights there—the Bellagio is beautiful and I've already booked a suite—"

"Wait a minute," she said. "You've *already* booked a suite? Pretty damned confident, aren't you?" She was trying to sound indignant, but her eyes and the laughter in them gave her away.

"I told you, I wasn't taking no for an answer. Not this time." He reached for her left hand. The ring looked beautiful there, just as though it had been made especially for her. "Anyway, there's no waiting period in Nevada." He smiled into her eyes. "So what do you say?"

"I do," P.J. said.

"I do," Alex said.

"I now pronounce you husband and wife," the Justice of the Peace said. He smiled at Alex. "You may kiss your bride."

P.J., thrilled beyond measure, kissed Alex with all her heart. The kiss lasted so long, the J.P. cleared his throat and said, "Ahem."

Laughing, Alex broke the kiss. Then, arms around each other, they thanked the J.P. and his wife, who had been their witness, and said goodbye.

Ten minutes later, tucked into the back

of a limousine, they held hands and kissed over and over again and marveled over the fact they really were Mr. and Mrs. Alexander Hunt.

Forever.

P.J. sighed.

She was the luckiest woman in the world.

## *Epilogue*

*New Year's Eve Day...*

"Nervous?" Alex asked.

"A little," P.J. admitted. "What do you think he'll say?"

"Don't know. Really don't care."

But P.J. knew Alex did care what his father thought. They were on their way to break the news that they were married. Alex wouldn't admit it for the world, because he would never want her to think he regretted marrying her, but she knew he hoped his father would back down on their agreement and accept her as Alex's wife without penalizing either him or his brothers.

They didn't have long to wait. They were almost to the Shack, as Alex wryly referred to his father's mansion overlooking Lake Washington.

P.J. had seen photos of the place, but even that didn't prepare her for the reality of its size. It was mammoth. "Holy cow," she said. "Your father really *lives* here?"

"Afraid so. It's disgustingly vulgar, isn't it?"

"Actually, it's beautiful, but who needs a place this big?"

"My sentiments exactly," Alex said. He pulled into the front turnaround and parked there.

P.J. knew his father was expecting Alex. He wasn't expecting her, because Alex had only said he was bringing someone with him and not who that someone was. Would Harrison Hunt have guessed it might be a woman? P.J. had no idea. She had butterflies in her stomach as they climbed the shallow stone steps leading to the enormous carved walnut double entrance doors.

A young maid dressed in black and wearing a white apron opened the doors at Alex's ring. She smiled tentatively. She looked as scared as P.J. felt and like P.J., was pretending she wasn't. P.J. gave her a sympathetic smile. She imagined it might not be easy to work for Alex's father.

"Mr. Hunt is expecting you," the maid said.

"Thank you," Alex said.

They were shown into a very formal living room. To P.J., the brocades and velvets and heavy dark furniture, the ornate paintings and many sculptures seemed cold. She almost shivered. She knew Alex was feeling the same way. Slipping her hand into his, she gave it a squeeze. When he looked down at her and smiled, she whispered, "I love you."

"I love you, too."

They sat close together on one of the dark-blue brocade sofas. Alex kept a tight hold on her hand.

A moment later, footsteps sounded in the hallway, and seconds later, a very tall man entered the room. P.J. would have recognized Harrison Hunt anywhere. First of all, she'd seen numerous pictures of him. Secondly, she'd always thought he bore an uncanny resemblance to the actor Jeff Goldblum. Older, of course, but strikingly similar.

Alex, still holding her hand, rose at his father's entrance.

"Well, well," Harrison Hunt said. "What have we here?" He directed his laser-like gaze to P.J.

P.J. held herself tall, with her chin up.

"Dad," Alex said, "This is P.J." He waited a beat. "My wife."

If Harrison Hunt was surprised, he hid it well. "Is that so?"

Extricating her hand from Alex's, P.J. stepped forward. "Hello, Mr. Hunt." She held out her right hand.

He took it, giving it a strong shake. P.J. returned it in kind. He examined her face carefully. "And how long have you been married to my son?"

She smiled proudly. "Three days."

"P.J.'s the daughter of Peter Prescott Kincaid," Alex said. "I met her at our distribution center. She manages the floor."

Finally Alex had managed to elicit a reaction from his father, for Harrison Hunt was visibly taken aback. "You're Peter's daughter?"

"Yes," she said.

"And you work for *me?*"

"Yes."

"Why?"

"Because I wanted to succeed on my own merits, and because I don't like the corporate world."

A huge smile broke over the older man's face. "I've known your father for many years. He's a good man."

"Yes, he is."

Clapping Alex on the back, Harrison said, "This calls for champagne. Has Cornelia met your bride yet?"

"We're going over there when we leave here," Alex said, "but first, we have something else to tell you. You may not like this, but whether you do or not makes no difference to me…to us."

Alex's father frowned.

P.J. took a deep breath. This was something she needed to do. "I know about Alex's and his brothers' agreement with you, Mr. Hunt. Unfortunately, I probably cannot have children. I wish I could, but several specialists have said there's only a slim chance I can ever become pregnant."

Alex put his arm around her. "It doesn't matter to me. We intend to adopt."

Hearing the firm commitment in his voice, P.J. knew she had never loved him more than she did at this moment.

"How you build your family isn't important to me, either," Harrison said. "I'm just glad you want one." His smile was rueful. "And I hope you'll be a much better father to your children than I was to you."

Alex's smile was slow in coming, and P.J. heard the catch in his voice as he said, "You did your best."

"It wasn't good enough," Harrison said. He turned his gaze to P.J. "You'll keep *him* on the straight and narrow, though, won't you?"

P.J. chuckled. "Absolutely."

"Come here, my dear," Harrison said. "Let me give you a proper hug. And welcome to our family."

After a warm hug and a kiss on the cheek, Harrison said, "Let's go into my study. We'll have our champagne there and you can tell me all about yourself, P.J. And Alex? Nothing you've told me today affects the foundation or your brothers. As far as I'm concerned, you've fulfilled your part of our bargain." He smiled at P.J. again. "And I'd say you've fulfilled it extremely well."

Later, as they drove away, P.J. said, "Alex, since you didn't buy me a Christmas present…" She held up her left hand so she could see her rings sparkle in the sunlight. "Engagement and wedding rings don't count…there's something I really want."

Smiling over at her, Alex said, "Anything. Just name it."

"I want you to take me to meet your

mother. I think it's time you mended that fence, too, don't you?"

He didn't answer for a few seconds, and she thought he was going to say no.

"I won't take no for an answer," she teased. "I'll keep after you until you finally say yes."

"You won't have to," he finally said, tenderness and love in his voice. "You know what? Today, listening to my father, seeing how he's trying to change, I thought the same thing. It's past time to forgive my mother. Way past time."

And that was the moment P.J. knew that no matter what life might throw at them in the future, they would be able to handle it.

They were a team.

For better, for worse, for richer, for poorer, in sickness and in health, till death do them part, they were a team.

\* \* \* \* \*

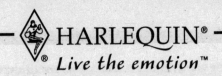

## Harlequin® Historical
### Historical Romantic Adventure!

*Imagine a time of chivalrous knights and unconventional ladies, roguish rakes and impetuous heiresses, rugged cowboys and spirited frontierswomen— these rich and vivid tales will capture your imagination!*

*Harlequin Historical . . . they're too good to miss!*

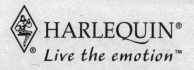

# HARLEQUIN®
# INTRIGUE®

## BREATHTAKING ROMANTIC SUSPENSE

Shared dangers and passions lead to electrifying
romance and heart-stopping suspense!

Every month, you'll meet six new heroes
who are guaranteed to make your spine tingle
and your pulse pound. With them you'll enter
into the exciting world of Harlequin Intrigue—
where your life is on the line
and so is your heart!

## THAT'S INTRIGUE—
## ROMANTIC SUSPENSE
## AT ITS BEST!

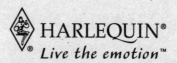

HARLEQUIN®
*Live the emotion*™